Slightly Spooky Stories I

Patsy Collins

To my stepmum Fi
(Even though she's not at all scary or ghostlike.)

Table of Contents

1. Telling The Truth

I'd had a rotten day at work; all I wanted to do was sling something in the microwave for tea and slump in front of the television. The *Ghost Buster* song blared. I didn't answer, just switched my phone to silent.

"Don't bring that in here," Justin said, pointing at my mobile.

"Why not?" I asked.

"Because of the electro-magnetic field."

"What are you on about now?"

"All electronic equipment generates a magnetic field. That's what's keeping the ghosts away. It makes sense; ghosts were much more common years ago. Technology is stopping them get through," he said.

"Even if that's true, the phone won't make much of a difference. The computer must give off a bigger charge," I said as I walked into my lounge. My TV, computer and stereo were gone. I didn't trust myself to speak, so headed for the kitchen. I saw a dusty space where my microwave once stood. That's when I decided the man must go.

What had possessed me to get involved with him? I'd rowed with Owen, I remembered, although I couldn't remember what about. Owen is not much to look at and you can't honestly say he's got a great body. In these respects, Justin is far superior. Unfortunately, his attraction is only skin deep. He only cares about ghosts and the supernatural. These subjects interest me too, but I don't prefer dead people to my family and friends. Justin does.

The only time we'd sat staring into each other's eyes was when he tried telepathy. Fortunately, that didn't work. He asked endless questions about the ghosts he believed live here. The only way to get rid of him was to tell him they don't exist. That was going to be awkward, especially after I'd attracted him by claiming the cottage was haunted.

"So where's all my stuff?" I asked.

"In the garage. I'll get a charity shop to collect it."

"There's no need."

"Yes there is. I explained. Weren't you listening?"

"Justin, there's no need because there are no ghosts."

"Of course there are," he said.

"Really? Prove it."

Justin pointed to the article he was writing. I remembered then what the argument with Owen had been about. I'd wanted to tell people about my haunted house. Owen hadn't thought it a good idea, but Justin had been very enthusiastic.

I read over Justin's shoulder.

"Anyone could make up things like that," I said.

"But it was you who told me most of it," he pointed out.

"Sorry, but I was making it up."

"What about the tape?" he tapped the recording he'd made of late night wailing.

I opened a drawer and produced my own tape.

"I set the stereo on a timer."

"And these?" He held up the photos.

"Just a bunch of pictures of an empty room."

"There was a ghost there when I took them."

"No, that was me wrapped in old rags. I deleted the

pictures of me and took more of nothing at all."

Justin left soon after that.

I telephoned Owen, leaving a message which I hoped would explain everything. I hadn't seen Owen since Justin moved in. Hardly surprising really.

I missed him a lot. Whilst I waited impatiently for the hoped for call from Owen, I cleared up the dust which had accumulated behind my appliances. I rescued the stereo from the garage; the rest could wait until I had help. I almost dropped a speaker when my phone rang. It was Owen.

"So you've kicked the new boyfriend out and want the old one to come running back?" he asked.

"Owen, I'm sorry we argued. You were right, but not about him being my boyfriend. He wasn't interested in me at all. He slept in the spare room."

"You were interested in him though."

I took a deep breath; it was time to stop lying. "I suppose I was. I'm not any more. You're the one I really want."

"Shall I come round then, so we can talk about it?"

My spine tingled at the thought of seeing him again. "Yes please, Owen," I said and switched off the phone.

"So you've seen sense at last, dearie?" an old lady's voice asked.

I looked at the head sticking through my wall.

"Yes, Ethel, I have." She smiled and wriggled the rest of her body through the brickwork. Her husband rose up through the wooden floor to join her.

"Perhaps you'll listen to our advice now."

As I waited for Owen, they gave me some tips to ensure that Owen and I would live, and die, happily ever after.

2. Spirit Of The Château

The boy is dressed all in black. His loose trousers and shapeless top are black. Even his footwear is black. I suppose he is a boy; at my age anyone under thirty seems young. His hair is long and dark. It moves, gently blown by a breeze I cannot feel. His face is pale, too pale for summer, for health. He looks sad, lost. I follow as he wanders around the château. I cannot hear his footsteps echoing through the empty rooms. His feet don't seem to touch the same floorboards that I walk upon. He has a hazy indistinct appearance, as if not quite of my world. I shake my head, I'm being fanciful; the sad reason for this visit is clouding my imagination.

I think I've seen him before; I may have done. There was a boy born here, a cousin of mine. No, that was too long ago, perhaps this is his son? I've visited so often, seen so many people, that it's difficult to remember. People and events are confused in my memory. Time passes quickly now, a whole summer goes by and seems no more than a few warm days. People I remember as laughing children, picnicking in the gardens or rowing on the lake are now grey, or gone.

My early years are clearer, my happy childhood spent in this château, the ponies I rode in the grounds. I remember friends and the games we played. I remember the handsome young woman I became, my love affairs and heartbreaks. Grand parties were held here, in this very ballroom. The gilding is peeling from the walls now. The once glittering chandelier was removed years ago. I hope it sparkles from another ceiling.

The boy moves toward the sweeping staircase and ducks under the coloured tape that warns the structure is now unsafe. He seems to care nothing for the potential danger. Perhaps he feels, as I do, that the château can never harm those who love it. I see him in profile as he turns. I was right; he is one of the family. Men who were my ancestors had a nose like that, eyebrows just like his. I've seen their portraits. They were bigger, more substantial men than this boy. Their smiling faces watching me from the canvas seemed more alive than this slim, pale child. He is one of us though; those features will be carried through my family for generations to come.

I remember him now, how could I have forgotten the little boy who occasionally wandered this very hallway at midnight? He crept quietly, keeping to the shadows, looking for something he never found. His disappointed face saddened me whenever I caught a glimpse of it.

He does love this place. I see that now as he slides his hand over the cracked wooden panelling. I know he is trying to see the fine detail gleaming with centuries of care and polish. That's how I see it, the beauty, the magnificence is still there, just beneath the neglected surface.

I have to concentrate to keep the present and not the past before my eyes. I remember the luxurious furniture that once graced these empty rooms. I can almost feel the warmth from the open fires, although I know the grates hold nothing but fallen soot and accumulated litter. The echo of voices is faint now. To anyone but those who love this old decayed château there is nothing here but crumbling plaster, rotten wood, and weakened bricks. To them it won't matter that men will come tomorrow to demolish my old home. Perhaps they're right, it doesn't really matter, wherever I am, I will still have my happy memories.

The boy is in the bedroom that was once mine. He looks up. Sun streams through the hole in the roof. He looks away from the light and into the shadows; looking for something. Surely, he knows everything of value was taken long ago. Since then the curious, the homeless, the lovers seeking privacy have walked through every room, searched every secret corner. There's nothing here but my memories, my love for this place and now, the boy. He walks to where the window once was. The glass slipped and fell so long ago, the frame shortly afterwards. I smile, recalling the mornings I'd leapt from bed and thrown open the heavy curtains to see what kind of day I would have. There were the Christmas mornings, when I longed for snow. There had been long summers with skies of unbroken blue. There had been rain and wind and sun, but always joy.

The boy turns to face me, his eyes widen and then he smiles. I know that he sees what he sought. He sees me; the spirit of the château.

"I'm glad to know you're real," he whispers.

"Of course I'm real, why did you doubt that?"

"Because although I heard all the stories, I never saw you. Whenever I stayed here as a child I'd stay up late, hoping you'd appear, but you never did."

"I was here."

"Then why didn't I see you?"

"The living often can't see us."

Together we take a last look around the château that had, in life, been our home, then we leave to join our ancestors.

3. Lucky Charm

"Lucky charm this, mate," the stallholder said.

He offered me a small dark object. It slipped from his hand and I caught it without thinking. It felt warm.

"Antique, probably," he encouraged.

"What is it?" I asked.

"Flower vase I suppose. It brings luck; well, it did for Mum."

Surely he couldn't expect people to be so gullible? "If it's so lucky I'm surprised she can bear to part with it." My tone was more than a little sarcastic.

"She's dead."

"Oh. I'm sorry," I said. I was too. I've acquired the knack of upsetting everyone.

"That's OK, mate. You weren't to know."

I noticed the price, only £3. I bought it. I'd no need of such a thing, but it seemed the best way of apologising. The seller offered to keep it safe until I left the boot sale.

I walked round without much interest. Most of the items were little more than rubbish. I didn't try to speak to anyone. Whenever I utter a sentence, I have to immediately apologise. It's been that way since I returned to England.

Marjorie and I went to Spain after my retirement. We knew she wasn't strong. The warmth helped a little and we had four very happy years there. The end, when it came, was swift. I thought I was prepared; but I felt so lost, so alone, without her. The isolation was entirely my fault. All our friends were really her friends. I'd spent my time reading English newspapers and playing bowls with other ex-pats. I'd condescended to drink the local wine and enjoy the weather but never considered the place home. I never learnt the language, no point I reasoned when so many people spoke English. What a pompous, arrogant fool I was.

I didn't improve when I returned home. I didn't have a home here of course, but at sixty-nine, had quite a few years left and must live them somewhere. I bought a pleasant little bungalow, a few minutes' walk from the sea. Marjorie had worried I'd become a recluse; I'd vowed to make friends and develop interests. I tried. It wasn't easy. During her illness, I learnt to cook and clean so I imagined I'd cope. I didn't realise that without her I wouldn't want to.

Joining the local bowls club helped. Exercise is a tonic, of course. So is company. Once people realised I was a widower, I received invitations to meals. I took bottles of Spanish wine and was careful not to stay too long, so these occasions have been fairly successful.

I started visiting the local church, mostly for the hymns and the warm welcome. A couple invited me in for a sherry after the service. It became a regular habit and I declared as I once lived in the country that produced it, I should provide the sherry. Providing drinks eases my conscience, for I accept all invitations, but issue none. I think most of my hosts understand and are happy with this arrangement.

Over sherry, I was introduced to a lady I'd seen regularly in church, yet never spoken to.

"Mrs Halibut, what a pleasure to be o-fish-ally introduced," I said.

"It's Harley, as in the motorcycle. Hyphen. Butt, as in

target for ridicule."

"Ah. Sorry, my mistake."

"It was my late husband's name. Today would have been his birthday."

I have since met Mrs Harley-Butt several times. The first meeting was probably the most successful. Once I spilt wine on her. Once I asked when her grandchild was due, later learning her daughter was simply overweight. Realising I was thinking of the lady because I'd heard a voice exactly like hers. I abruptly changed direction.

My face was stiff with cold, my eyes streaming and my shoes caked with mud. I decided to claim my vase and leave.

"There you go, mate. Wrapped nice and safe. D'you want a bag?"

"Please."

"Hope it brings you more luck than it did me."

"Oh."

"Mum swore it brought her luck, but she said you had to appreciate it, or it would do you no good. Bought two lottery tickets I did and stood the vase on top of them."

"Your numbers didn't come up."

"Oh, they came up all right, three on one line, three on t'other. Millions I should have got, not just twenty."

"Oh dear."

"Not just that. Nipped across the road a bit sharpish one day and whose car should catch me, but the mayor's."

"Were you badly hurt?"

"Not a mark, not even dust on me trousers. Think of the compensation I lost out on."

I nodded sympathetically.

"Mum left me some money too, so I spent a bit on the car. My old banger was always packing up and with the missus expecting, I had it properly serviced and joined the AA. Waste of money that was. Up for renewal the membership is and I've not used it once."

"How annoying."

"And to cap it all, the wife who was supposed to produce the son and heir has just had twin girls. That's why I'm here selling all I can. Need to make money and space for another cot."

Strangely, after hearing his sad tale I felt a little happier. I considered that as I returned to my car. I wasn't lucky, but at least I wasn't as unfortunate as that poor fellow.

Through the sleet on my windscreen, I saw Mrs Harley-Butt arrive at the bus stop; just as the bus pulled away. So, it really was her voice I'd heard. I pulled up and offered her a lift.

"My conversation and manners may be doubtful, but I'm a careful driver and the car has an excellent heater," I assured her.

Surprisingly we conversed politely enough on the journey. She told me she visited the car boot sale about once a month. On those weeks she attended the evening church service. "Actually I prefer it, more singing, less sermons."

It occurred to me I might prefer the evening service for the same reason.

"If you are thinking of going tonight I would be pleased to offer transport," I said.

"Oh no, I don't want to put you out."

"I'd be glad of the outing. Evenings are so lonely."

We travelled for a time without speaking, we didn't know

each other well enough to continue the conversation. When we spoke again, we discussed the car boot sale. She had been looking for frames as she made tapestry pictures. It was cheaper to buy old prints, throwing out the pictures, than to by a new frame. She enjoyed the challenge of adapting designs to the varied shapes and styles.

I began to tell her of my purchase as we neared the village.

"Could you please drop me at the Crown and Sceptre? I'll have my lunch there."

"Lunch?" I hadn't thought about lunch, mine would have to be a cheese sandwich.

"They do a lovely roast, with proper Yorkshires."

"Sounds good."

"The car park is that way."

I admired the way she arranged things, avoiding the awkwardness of inviting me to join her. Wine was served by the glass. Mrs Harley-Butt allowed me to buy her a glass of sweet white. I chose a good rich Rioja. The meal was as good as she promised. A choice of beef, lamb or pork was offered, with roast and new potatoes and seasonal vegetables. I selected the lamb after being told I could still have a Yorkshire pudding if we smiled at the waitress. The food was nicely presented, with a large jug of hot gravy and the vegetables in a separate dish. Carrots, cauliflower, broccoli and mini corn cobs jostled for position. It seemed a lot of food, but I didn't expect we'd leave any.

"My name's Millie by the way."

"Donald."

"Cheers, Donald."

We raised glasses.

"You were telling me about your lucky charm. If it's so lucky why would anyone sell it?"

"Exactly what I asked."

I related what had happened to the stall holder since he'd owned the vase.

"So it's true. It really is lucky," Millie said.

"Do you think so?"

"As soon as the man got it he won £20, he survived an accident without injury, his previously unreliable car has worked perfectly for a year and he now has two healthy daughters."

"I see what you mean. His mother considered it was only lucky for those who appreciated their luck. Obviously he didn't."

"I wonder if it will be lucky for you."

"Perhaps it is working already." I was surprised to find my mood was optimistic. "I had expected a cheese sandwich for lunch and a lonely evening. Instead, I'm enjoying your company, delicious food and have plans for the evening. That's if you do want a lift."

"I do, thank you. The treacle tart here is as good as the roast potatoes."

Again, she was right.

The vase stayed in the car, it was out of sight and so I didn't remember to take it into the house. When anything good happened, I remembered it though. One of my premium bonds gained me £50. Millie and I heard of a concert we wished to attend, it was sold out but they took my number and phoned on the day to report a cancellation. My annual medical showed my health to be excellent.

Millie and I became good friends, it was understood that

we were not looking for romance. We both wanted company, someone to spend a day out with, a meal, a joke, occasionally a tear.

The church was warmer than the muddy field of the car boot sale, so we went there most Sunday mornings over the winter. As spring approached, Millie wanted a new picture frame. It was not until I called to collect her for the trip I remembered my vase was still in the car. Millie asked to see it. Once unwrapped I realised it was not the one I had bought. The one I held was glass with lead beading representing a flower.

"It might be the wrong one, but I think it's beautiful," Millie said.

"Then please accept it as a gift."

We noticed the price tag; £5. The man had not tried to cheat me, but simply made a mistake. He had been packing up I remembered, and the shape was similar.

At the sale, I saw the man who sold it to me. He no longer had a stall but was with his family, hunting for bargains. He remembered me.

"I'd better give you your money back, mate."

"On the contrary I owe you £2."

"Can't take that, mate, and you can't have the vase you tried to buy either. Sorry but I should never have tried to sell it."

"Oh?"

"Once you'd gone I thought about what I'd said. Two beautiful little girls I've got here, and there was I thinking I'd no luck."

He introduced us to his cheerful wife and we tried to admire the babies. That was difficult to do through the blankets, hats, gloves and scarves but we made appropriate comments.

"I thought about what me mum said and I figured I'd been looking at things wrong. The next week when I set up the stall I was pleased to see I still had it, but hoped you wouldn't think I'd swindled you."

I assured him I realised it was an honest mistake.

"Then I saw I'd wrapped it in the job section of the paper. The price tag stuck onto one ad. I'd been made redundant you see. Makes you lose your nerve. Still, I thought it was a sign. The job was for a fork lift truck driver. I used to do that so I rang up. They'd had the interviews but the bloke they chose never showed up. I started the same day. Mum was right, there's plenty of luck; you just have to look out for it."

4. Mad As Hell

Her head tilted on one side, she scurries down the narrow street towards me, shouting angrily at no one.

"Leave me alone."

She looks back over her shoulder but there is nothing to see. Her miss-buttoned jacket does little to protect her from the damp, penetrating cold. The scarf that had been flapping around her falls but, apparently, is not missed. I note where it lands so I can collect it when she's gone. Her high heeled cream shoes and that thin, short skirt with bare legs are hardly suitable for a walk at this time of night.

"Leave me alone, I don't want to listen," she snarls out to the east wind.

Onwards she stumbles, picking her way around puddles and discarded chip wrappers. The large heavy bag that is constantly slipping from her shoulder is dragged back into position. Again, she looks over her shoulder but there is nothing; just the street and the cold and me. I'm nothing now, but I used to be a real person once. I had a home and a family, but that was before.

Her fidgety hands pull uneasily at her hair, then adjust the collar of her jacket. Loudly sniffing she runs her hand across her nose and the bag slithers once more from her shoulder. Angrily she hoists it up and steps onto a discarded carrier bag. Her left leg slides forward and she crashes to the ground. In the awkward position she has landed she stays, and sobs.

"Stop it. It's your fault... I hate you, leave me alone... leave me alone."

Occasionally looking behind her, she just waits there in silence unwilling or unable to find the motivation to continue. Breathing heavily, gasping as the icy air is drawn into her body she begins to cry. Her hands gathered to her face she whimpers about her pain.

"Your fault... your fault... Why can't you just leave me alone?" She wants answers, to be able to understand her anguish.

"Why...? Why?"

The wind doesn't reply, nor do the deserted offices, the apartments above remain silent, their occupants now in dreamless sleep. There is no one to hear, no one to care or understand on these streets. Out here, there is no answer. She looks behind her once more but remains alone.

Eventually staggering to her feet, she gathers her possessions together. The left shoe retrieved from the half-eaten, long cold kebab. Oblivious of the pungent chilli sauce and shredded cabbage she thrusts her grazed foot back in. As she rushes on, her arms are wrapped about her, holding her head and clutching at the now filthy strap of her bag.

"I'm not listening," her voice echoing in the empty street. "No you don't... I don't care... you don't... just leave me alone."

She goes on, past the closed shops and empty pub. Even the Indian restaurant is dark and silent now, only the unmistakable smell of coriander hinting at its earlier Friday night crowds. Past the church now, her head twisted away from its locked oak doors and shadowed windows. She looks behind again but sees not the crucifix nor sign promising a warm welcome, only an empty street.

Abruptly stopping, the girl places her bag at her feet and straightens up. She listens.

"No you don't... You can't mean it... You don't mean it."

She's quieter now subdued. Tired I suppose.

"I'm sorry too," she whispers.

"I'll come home then, shall I?" She switches off her mobile phone and picking up her bag, turns and walks back the way she came.

I watch until she's out of sight, then dart out to grab her dropped scarf and wrap it round my neck. It's clean and soft and warm, the nicest thing I own. Wearing it, I retreat into my cardboard bed in the draughty doorway. Maybe one day I too will get the chance to say sorry and go home. Maybe.

5. Brainwashing Barbara

Barbara stared at the group of youths smoking outside the snooker club. "Why would they do that?"

"No choice these days."

"Of course they have a choice," Barbara snapped. Her irritation was more at herself than her friend. Barbara hadn't meant to ask her question aloud. "They don't have to get tattoos or wear those ridiculous trousers which don't stay up, or smoke just because everyone else does. It's as though they've been brainwashed."

"I just meant about doing it outside, because of the smoking ban," Martha explained.

"I know about that, I'm not senile you know."

"Of course not."

Oh dear, she'd snapped again. "I'm sorry, Martha. I don't know what's wrong with me lately. I've been on edge for a while now. To be honest, I'm worried."

"Let's go and get a coffee and you can tell me about it."

"I think I would like a coffee."

Sitting with the hot mug cupped in her hands and a slice of sponge cake in front of her, Barbara felt a lot better. The restlessness in her fingers and the feeling there was something she should be doing was temporarily gone.

"What's bothering you?" her friend asked.

"I don't know… I just have a feeling something is wrong, or missing… it's hard to explain. I've been short with people and I've had a bit of a headache sometimes, but I don't know if that's why I'm worried, or I'm worrying because of that."

"That sounds natural enough. I expect it will pass."

"Do you think so?" It was a relief to hear Martha say that; she was always the sensible, health conscious one.

Barbara took a sip of coffee. "Gosh, this is good!"

"Try the cake."

Barbara did. "Mmmm, they must make this with butter, and the jam in the middle is gorgeous. Why on earth did we stop coming here?"

"You said there was no point."

"I did?" Maybe there really was something wrong with her. It must have been going on far longer than she'd realised too; they'd not been to the tea rooms for ages. "Oh!" It was coming back to her. Everything had just tasted the same so it seemed pointless to spend several pounds each on coffee and cakes out when she could make them cups of instant and open a box at home.

"They must have got a new manager or something."

Martha tried to suppress a smile. People had been doing that around her a lot lately. It wasn't quite that they were laughing at her, but as though they knew she wouldn't get the joke and wanted to avoid having to explain it. Her daughter and son-in-law were just the same. At times they seemed to be humouring her and she was almost positive that once or twice her grandchildren had deliberately been silenced before they could say something they shouldn't.

"You'd tell me if I was ill, wouldn't you?" As soon as Barbara asked, she realised it was a daft question. Martha would be the first person to do that. It was she who'd started them on their daily walks. "You've got to use it or lose it at our age," she'd said. When they were younger, much, much younger, it was Martha who'd advised her against silly fad diets and all manner of reckless behaviour.

"Do you feel ill?" Martha asked.

"Not now, but I was a few weeks ago. For a few days I was really shaky, my head throbbed and I felt sick. That's when I was staying at my Lynne's."

Martha nodded to show she remembered.

"It's such a shame. Usually I love being with them all. I try to make up for her fussing over me by babysitting, so she and John get a couple of nights out on their own. Well, that's my excuse. Really I just like the chance to get my gorgeous grandchildren to myself and spoil them a bit. That time though, I was a real misery."

"I'm sure they'll all understand."

"That's what everyone keeps saying! Something happened about six weeks ago, didn't it? Something I can't remember?"

"I can see I'm going to have to explain, but before I do will you answer me some questions?"

"Do I have a choice?"

Martha grinned. "Not with this! First, are you feeling better than when you were at Lynne's?"

"Yes, much."

"Better than before that?"

"I don't know… in some ways I suppose."

"For instance you're not getting so out of breath on our walks?"

"No, I'm not." Was that what she felt was missing from her life? Her wretched cough and the need to keep stopping to catch her breath?

"And your appetite?" Martha indicated Barbara's empty cake plate.

"Better, I'm really enjoying my food these days." She was looking less as though all the goodness had been sucked out of her too.

"How about money? Are you worried about that?"

"Martha, that's it! Money has been on my mind... I seem to have too much. The last few days before I got my pension were always a real struggle, but now I have some left over."

"That's good."

"Not really. There must be a bill or something I've forgotten about. But if I can just work out what I should be spending that money on, I can stop worrying about it. Thank you, you've relieved my mind a little."

"Good. Let's pay the bill here and go and buy cigarettes then."

"What?" Maybe it was Martha's state of mind she should be worrying about, not her own? "Why would we do such a stupid thing?"

"Buying a pack every day will take care of your spare money. I believe they cost over £5."

"Yes, £8.24. Oh! How would I know that?"

"Because until six weeks ago you were a smoker. Your daughter took you to a hypnotist to get you cured. He convinced you you'd never smoked and we've all had to act as though that was true until you were over the worst of the withdrawal. You are now, aren't you?"

"I believe so."

She was. Thanks to the help of her friends, family and a little brainwashing, Barbara never smoked again.

6. Luck Dragon

Even in the faded book, the dragon was vital; alive. Energy seeped from the image. Dragons are powerful. Now no mythical saints remain to slay them, they're invincible. I wanted that strength. I craved fear and respect and if it was not freely given, I'd take it, just as years ago, I'd taken the book.

I'd wanted the tattoo done right away and soon stole the money to pay for it. I was a small lad then, too small for the old dears with their half open handbags to distrust me. Too small for the tattoo parlours to touch me without proof of the age I hadn't yet reached.

I waited, not patiently, but I waited; until I was eighteen.

"You do custom work?" I asked the shrunken yellow-skinned remains of the man in the tattoo parlour.

"Anything you want," he said without raising his bowed head to meet my gaze. I wanted to pull his plait of hair back, sharp and hard to force him to look at me. I didn't, I needed him.

"I'll have that." I touched the dry paper and thrust the book toward him.

"The luck dragon?"

"You know what it is?"

"I know. A brave choice."

"You think getting a tattoo is brave, old man?"

"Getting that tattoo is. There is more than one kind of luck you know."

"I know."

How could I not? There is the luck you were born with and the luck you make for yourself. I'd only ever had the one kind. I'd been a welfare kid; free school meals and hand-me-down clothes. A charity paid for my seat on the trip to the museum. The other kids could buy sweets, but stole them anyway. They wanted the cash for fags. Silly brats; why take the risk for toffee, when there were treasures within reach? I took the book and waited. I waited until no one would dare to doubt I was a man.

The Chinaman who scarred and inked my flesh didn't question me. He barely touched me, the only sensation was that of the needle etching its way across my back. He advised against having the whole thing done in one go.

I advised him to keep working.

It was night when he finished, but even in the feeble artificial light the dragon was clear and vivid. It curled around my back, the tip of its tail above my right hip, the flames from its mouth flickering over my left shoulder. It glowed vital; alive. Though I didn't tell the old man, his work was better than the image in the now fading book.

"What luck will it bring?"

"Depends how you pay," the old fool smirked at me.

He hoped my superstition would match his greed and the price would be high. I paid as I always do; with hard fists and quick feet.

The dragon grows. I feel his strength within me. No longer must I live by the restricting rules that bind other men. No longer must I run from the consequences of my actions. I make my own luck now and my own rules. I am one with the dragon.

The dragon grows. We are invincible

The dragon grows. The dragon is invincible.

The dragon grows. He is unstoppable.

Unstoppable.

His hot breath sears my chest, blazes in my belly. The weight of his body bows mine. I don't have the strength to hold him. I run my hands over my torso and feel the throb of his pulse as his blood is pumped into my veins. The dragon's scales form from my flesh, their smooth ripple distorting my sore, dry skin. Talons dig into me; I feel them as I move. The dragon's thoughts are pushed into my mind and dragon's breath burns through my blood. The dragon gains power and I weaken.

I find the jaundiced Judas. He etched the dragon onto my skin; he must remove it from my soul.

"I'll pay you this time."

"Yes, lad, you will pay. You'll pay the ultimate price."

With cold steel, he slices my wrists. I watch as the dragon's blood seeps from my veins. I am too weak now to hold the book the old man offers. As he turns the pages, I recognise it as the one I left behind on my first visit. He shows me the page I once showed him.

The dragon again glows vital; alive.

7. Working in the Bookshop

I nearly didn't bother when I saw the woman at the counter. Didn't think she'd like the look of me. For one thing I'm a big lad, almost six four, and Brookes' bookshop is tiny. Old ladies generally look as though they'd like to tell me to pull my trousers up, my hood down and remove the rings and studs. They never do; other than Gran they usually just try to ignore me. Still, I needed a job and the shop needed staff so I stood patiently as the old lady served a customer.

"Can I help you?" she said as though she wasn't at all sure that was likely.

I shrugged.

"Are you looking for a book?"

I shook my head.

"A card or gift?"

"Nah," I mumbled at the floor.

I'd have walked out except there was another old dear behind me and she seemed to be urging me to continue. I know that sounds weird, but it's what it felt like. Suddenly it seemed worth trying.

"I'm hoping I can help you," I said in the voice I used on Gran when I offered to cut us both another slice of her lemon drizzle cake. "I'm interested in the job."

The old lady's hand hovered over a file marked 'application forms'. "Do you have any experience?"

"Yes. I worked for a while at Blackwell's." That's true as

far as it goes. I did my school work experience there. Pretty much all I did was open boxes, read Andy McNab and Terry Pratchett novels and make tea, but still. What did she expect? I'd not left school that long before and there aren't jobs going anywhere, not for someone with zero qualifications.

"If you like I could do a month's trial." I have no idea why I said that. The idea just seemed to jump into my head.

"I'm not sure…"

While she was trying to think of an excuse a van pulled up outside and the driver jumped out with a clipboard in his hand.

"Looks like you've got a delivery," I said.

The boxes would have been heavy and awkward to manoeuvre for her but for me with my big hands and long arms it was easy. Once I'd stacked them up where she wanted them, she thanked me, gave me an application form and asked me to come back on Saturday for an interview.

I tried a few more shops in town but by the time I caught the bus home, I still only had the one application form.

When I told Gran about it she asked who I'd spoken to.

I shrugged. "Dunno."

"What did they look like, Matt?"

I nearly said it was an old dear, but stopped in time. "A tall lady, long hair in one of those knotted things, about your age."

"So, she's still there. Do you actually want this job, or are you going to turn up looking like that?"

"I do want it actually." Well, I wanted a job and this seemed my best chance, so I did all the stuff I knew old ladies always think I should do. Most of my jewellery was taken out, I pulled on my only non-black sweatshirt and brushed my hair off my face. I even borrowed a belt, but drew the line at letting Gran trim my fringe.

"You look so much better when you're not hiding behind all that stuff," she said. "Remember to speak instead of grunting and you'll be fine."

"What do I say?"

"Just tell the truth."

Without my hood I felt vulnerable sitting on the bus. No one spoke to me or anything though. Looking at my reflection in the window I wasn't convinced how I looked was any kind of improvement, but I suppose I did seem a bit more like someone who might work in a bookshop.

The lady who worked there seemed to think so too. Took her a moment to remember who I was. "Oh, you're the boy who helped with the delivery. I'll be with you in just a moment."

She put a sign on the door, then took me into a sort of office out the back.

"I am Miss Brookes. Do have a seat."

Miss Brookes, who I guessed must be the owner, looked through my application form and the references I'd brought with me. Both were from friends of Gran's and didn't say much other than they believed me to be trustworthy and reliable. I'd thought that was a bit rubbish, but Gran had said it would be OK.

"Do you have an interest in books, Matthew?"

"Yeah." Then I remembered what Gran said and told her who my favourite authors are.

"And why do you enjoy reading those books?"

"Because I can go to other places and do different things."

Then in case she thought I was stupid I added, "I know I'm not in the army or anything and that Discworld and all that are made up, but reading the books... it's like it's all real and I'm there."

"I see. And do you think you would like working for us?"

"Yeah. It's boring having nothing to do all day." I'd lost touch with my old friends, most of who were at college, my parents are at work in the day and pretty fed up with me anyway and I don't have any money. Obviously I didn't say all that. Despite how it might seem I'm really not stupid.

"We would need you to come in on Saturdays, but you could take off whichever day you choose during the week."

"OK." I'd guessed about working Saturdays.

"You mentioned a month's trial and I think that's a good idea."

"You'd pay me, right?"

"Yes, Matthew. I propose we employ you for a month and then if we decide you are suitable and you'd like to remain, we make it a permanent arrangement."

"OK and by the way, it's Matt usually."

"Then we shall look forward to seeing you on Monday, Matt."

It was a bit weird her talking like there was more than one of her, but old ladies often are a bit weird. Gran's obsessed with making lemon drizzle cake, but that's a good kind of weirdness. It wasn't until we were back in the shop that it hit me I had a job at last. Just for a second I was nervous, but then I had this feeling everything was going to be great.

Gran thought so too. "I know I never go there, but I like to think of Brookes' still running. So many of the shops I remember have been replaced by big chains now."

"Did you buy your slate there for school?" I don't exactly know what a slate is, but pretending I think she had one always gets a reaction from her.

"Don't be so cheeky or you'll get no cake!"

"Ooops. Your laptop is what I meant to say."

"Hmm."

Once I had a wedge of lemon drizzle and mug of coffee she admitted she did buy some school supplies at Brookes'. "I went to school with the daughters of the owners. Your Miss Brookes is a bit older than me and her sister a year younger. They loved the shop and ran it together after their father retired. Then there was a fire. Poor Beth was burned."

I understood my boss always talking like there was two of her after that. It was the same as Gran still making the lemon drizzle cakes Grandad used to love. There are some things people just don't want to admit, even to themselves.

For the first few days Miss Brookes was with me all the time, showing me what to do. She also encouraged me to read a lot. I was allowed to read for two hours a day in the shop, even if there were other things to do, and to take books home with me.

"As long as you're very careful. We can't afford to damage any stock."

Believe me, I was extremely careful.

"I expect they did a lot of things differently at Blackwells," she said.

"The tills were different," I said. Not that they'd let me near one, but I could see hers was a real old fashioned thing.

"I imagine so. With this one you'll have to calculate discounts and work out how much change is owed yourself."

"I can do that."

I soon proved that was true. By the end of the week I was serving customers while Miss Brookes worked in the office. I did go and ask her a few things for customers, but I was OK with most of it. After a week, Miss Brookes left me in charge while she had her lunch or went shopping. Soon it felt almost normal to look people in the face and smile at them and to not have a hood up and metalwork in. Sometimes I didn't bother putting it all back when I got home.

Brookes' just calls itself a bookshop but it sells all kinds of things. There's lots of stationery and cards and bows and toys and stuff for weddings and ornaments. It was hard for customers to find things sometimes, though often whatever I'd been asked for just seemed to appear. Not like it was beamed down, but the drawer I needed would be not quite shut or the box the thing was in would be slightly out of line so that was the first one I went to.

That sounds a bit creepy but it wasn't. The strange old lady was though. Actually no, not creepy but there was something about her. Not Miss Brookes I don't mean, but the other one. Although I'd not really seen her the first time, I was nearly sure it was the woman who'd seemed to urge me forward to ask about the job. She was definitely weird; never met my gaze and I couldn't exactly see her. Made me think of The Invisible Man. She wasn't see-through or anything but she was all covered up in old fashioned clothes. She always wore gloves and long skirts and sleeves. Her hair was over her face and she had thick make-up. I did wonder if she was a man.

Then I thought there might be more to it than that. She was there quite often, but not once did she buy anything. Mind you, we got a lot of that. People came in and read books in their lunch breaks or while waiting for the bus. One man even marked his page with a bookmark! He did sometimes buy cards though, according to Miss Brookes, so I didn't say anything. My month's trial wasn't up and I didn't want to risk upsetting a potential customer. I waited until he'd almost finished the book and then hid it under the counter. When he asked for it, I offered to order it in for him. He hesitated.

"It's a great story with a really well thought out ending." That's true by the way.

He paid up and I assured him we'd have it in very soon. As he left I was surprised to hear a woman chuckling as I'd not realised anyone else was there. It was the mystery woman.

She moved very quietly and I never noticed her arrive or leave. Odd that. The carpet was thick and there were lots of shelves and things meaning few places had a clear view of the door, but there was a little bell which dinged whenever it was opened. That never alerted me to her arrival.

The mystery woman seemed to spend most of her time in the draughty corner. Miss Brookes thought I was imagining the draught, because the old doorway had been properly sealed up, but sometimes I suddenly felt icy cold when I was there. Apparently there was once a separate little house, where they'd lived, through there.

"It burned down and rather than rebuild we sold the plot and created a flat over the shop," Miss Brookes told me. She gave a little frown. "When were you born?"

"March 1998."

"That's when it happened and it's had quite a few layers of paint since, not to mention having the optician's built against it. I assure you, nothing is coming in through there."

Remembering what Gran had told me about her sister and

the fire, I didn't mention the doorway again, but I did still feel the chill. Maybe the mystery woman didn't, under all her layers of clothes? That corner was the one where all the wedding stuff was. Confetti, party favours, lucky horse shoes, you know the kind of thing. I looked carefully after I'd seen her there but it didn't seem like she'd taken anything. I was glad of that as I couldn't have accused her of shoplifting even if I'd been sure she was guilty. All that stuff is cheap anyway. Books or pens are what anyone would go for, or the cash in the till. I really couldn't imagine she'd bash an assistant over the head and grab the takings, and was positive I'd be more than a match for her, or even him, if they tried.

The job came pretty easily to me. I learned a lot from Miss Brookes of course. She'd read almost every book we sold so could always advise customers on a suitable choice. I wasn't doing so badly myself. Sometimes when I was asked for a recommendation the answer almost leapt out at me. The cover might catch my attention or the title just appear in my head as though someone were whispering it to me. Just had the knack, I suppose. Although Miss Brookes had a massive head start, I was trying to catch up with her knowledge too.

Reading so many different books was putting ideas in my head I think. One of my theories was that the mystery lady was jilted at the altar. Unlike Miss Havisham in *Great Expectations*, who always wore her wedding dress, she had a compulsion to look at the knick-knacks people might have bought to take to her wedding. I felt a bit sorry for her then. Poor old thing had to be lonely, jilted or not. Why else was she hanging about in the bookshop?

When the man came in to buy the book he'd almost finished I told him there a free bookmark with it.

Neither of us mentioned that he'd put it there, but I heard the mystery lady laugh again when he'd gone out.

"You could make yourself useful you know," I said one day when I was unpacking a big delivery.

I kind of felt her being surprised, but after a moment she took a book from the pile I'd checked off and put it on the correct shelf. Then she took another and another. Between us we had the whole lot sorted by the time Miss Brookes was back from the dentist.

"Good gracious, Matt! You have been busy!"

The mystery woman was still there and even if it wasn't obvious then that I'd had help it would be when my boss did the cashing up and realised I'd had quite a few customers, so I admitted I'd not been working alone.

"Oh!"

Obviously she was a bit surprised that I'd roped in a customer to help, but she didn't actually say I shouldn't have done it. She didn't say much at all. Probably her tooth still hurt because she looked a bit unwell.

After that, the mystery woman spent even more time in the shop. She walked round pulling all the out of place books forward so they were lined up perfectly on the edges of the shelves and rearranged some of the displays. The draughty wedding corner got most of her attention. I'm not much good at fiddly stuff like that, but it did look better and we started selling a few more things.

"Matt, are you able to stay behind for a few minutes after we close today?" Miss Brookes asked one afternoon.

"Sure." I didn't need to ask why; I'd been working there exactly a month.

"How have you found working for us?" she asked when I

was sitting in her office.

"I like it here and I hope you'll keep me on."

"We shall. I'll admit that initially I had no intention of employing you, even after you kindly helped unload a delivery, but a few things swayed me, including references from two of my oldest friends."

Clever Gran! Bet she knew they were Miss Brookes' friends when she told me to ask them.

"Did you know my sister Beth was friends with Mary, your grandmother... before the accident?"

I nodded. Really what else could I do? Change the subject, that's what! "You said a couple of things swayed you?"

"Beth was the other."

"Oh." That hadn't gone how I'd planned.

"She wanted to give you a chance."

Taking staffing advice from a ghost is weird, but then so is getting one to help you with shelf stacking so I wasn't in a position to complain. "Maybe I reminded her of my gran?"

"Oh no, of herself." Miss Brookes seemed to be looking at someone else.

"You were hiding, Matt."

It wasn't Miss Brookes speaking. Well not the one who'd interviewed me anyway. I recognised the voice. It was the same one which had whispered book titles to me and chuckled when I'd made the bookmark man pay for a book he'd almost finished reading.

"I hide behind my make-up and hair and gloves... because of the scars. Just as you hid behind all that metal on your face and your black clothes."

"Yes." Gran always said that and she was right.

"I'm not going to hide any longer." Beth Brookes sat opposite me. I saw her hair was pulled back off her face and piled on her head and knotted up just like her older sister's. Her gloves, hat and scarf were gone, revealing skin more wrinkled and discoloured than you'd expect even on quite an old woman. She still wore some make-up, but it toned down rather than covered her scars. The result wasn't attractive, but neither was it repulsive.

"Working in the shop with you has helped me a lot," Beth Brookes said.

"It's helped me too," I admitted.

"I'd like to think we're friends, Matt. Just as I was friends with Mary."

"I'd like that too."

"Will you tell us what happened to her?" the older Miss Brookes asked.

I didn't think I could. I've not told anyone. Not my parents, not my teachers, not my friends. Ever since it happened I've shut myself away from everyone. Hiding just like she said. Somehow though I could tell the Brookes sisters.

"I killed her. Not on purpose but I killed her."

"Tell us."

So I did. I told them how I'd not finished the last book I'd been reading in Blackwell's when I did my work experience there. I couldn't afford to buy it, but I'd taken it home anyway. Gran had seen it and worked it out.

"Silly boy, Matt. If they find out you'll be in all sorts of trouble."

She took it back for me and on the way home she was knocked over. I visited her in hospital every day, but it was no good. She never came round.

By the time I'd finished the story a Brookes sister was holding each of my hands and I was dropping tears onto theirs; one wrinkled and scarred, one just wrinkled. I felt better though. I began to see that although Gran had died doing something for me, I hadn't actually killed her. I was able to think of her without guilt.

"One of the classes I took with Mary was cookery," Beth said after a long pause. "Lemon drizzle was our absolute favourite. Thinking of her prompted me to bake one this afternoon. Would you like a slice?"

You don't need me to tell you how I answered that.

8. Little Austin

Rob had almost forgotten about the Austin 7 until his dad rang up.

"Little Austin's been shut away in my lock-up for years while I've kidded myself I'll get round to restoring him. Reckon it's time to let someone else have a go. Want to try?"

As a boy, Rob had loved the car. He and his brother often sat in it as they were told the legends about Great Aunt Mabel saving mothers and babies against the odds. The boys had enjoyed hearing about Mabel's exploits especially when the stories involved the car. It got Mabel through storms, bombing raids and a fire. Even then Rob had thought it a shame the car was no longer used but left to rust in a draughty garage.

"I'd love it," Rob said. "But I'd better check with Helen. She's at her Zumba class now."

"Yes of course. How is she?"

"Fine."

She was, but just barely. She'd been so sure she was pregnant and so radiantly happy about it everyone guessed their news before the doctor disappointed them. Rob and Helen were more than disappointed. After twelve years of marriage those few joyful days had been the closest they'd come to being parents.

Helen wouldn't mind him restoring a vintage car, would probably enjoy helping him. Taking on a project like fixing up Little Austin might be good for them both. If only it had belonged to someone other than Great Aunt Mabel. The irony of using a car that had once helped mothers give birth being used to fill the empty lives of a childless couple wouldn't be lost on Helen. Would the car, or perhaps even the mention of it, upset her? Rob decided not to say anything, at least not for a while.

"What are you thinking about?" Helen asked him not an hour later.

Guessing that a secret might upset her more than hearing about the car, Rob explained he'd been offered Little Austin.

"Let's go take a look at it, see how much work it needs."

"Are you sure?"

"Yes. I know it'll probably prompt your dad to start talking about Great Aunt Mabel and all those babies, but everywhere I go there are babies, or pregnant women or..." Tears filled her eyes.

Rob held her close and stroked her back until she pulled away, blew her nose and gave a bright smile.

"My teacher's going to have to stop taking Zumba soon by the way, because she's pregnant. Isn't that lovely news?"

"Yes, lovely."

"Ring Dad then, see if we can go round now."

The car was in better condition than Rob had feared, though it clearly needed a lot of attention. He and his dad walked around it, noting what work was required. After a few minutes Rob realised Helen still stood in the garage doorway.

"All right, love?"

"You never said it was so beautiful."

"You like it, then?"

"I love it! Those wheels are so cute and so are the funny headlights and that colour is just gorgeous. We'll keep that won't we, when we repaint him?"

"Yes, if that's what you'd like."

"I would. I see why everyone calls him Little Austin now. He looks sort of friendly."

Rob's brother Richie borrowed a trailer and brought Little Austin home for them.

"I rather fancied restoring it myself," he admitted. "Maybe you'd let me help?"

Rob and Helen spent most weekends and many evenings working on Little Austin. The eagerness with which Helen pulled on her overalls and her satisfied grin at every small achievement were things Rob hadn't seen for some time. Richie came round to help fairly often too and soon they'd made quite good progress.

"Really looks the part now," Rob said to his wife one night. "Well, until anyone lifts the bonnet."

"True."

Rob frowned. Usually whenever there was the slightest suggestion the car wasn't perfect in every way, Helen jumped to Little Austin's defence. "Are you OK?"

"Absolutely."

"But?"

"There's no but. It's just, well, there's a chance I'm pregnant."

"Oh."

She smiled. "That's about what I thought. After last time I don't really feel able to react at all. Let's not talk about it and try not to think about it."

"OK. I'll try."

They didn't discuss the possibility, but Rob couldn't help hoping Helen was pregnant and he was fairly sure she barely thought about anything else.

"Can you get an hour off work," she asked one day. "To come to the doctor's with me?"

Rob just squeezed her hand and nodded.

Work continued on Little Austin throughout Helen's pregnancy, though at a much slower rate than previously. For the last week there was almost no progress at all, mostly because Rob wouldn't leave Helen's side in case 'something happened' but also because the weather was so bad the short walk to the garage was unappealing. Richie couldn't spare much time either now that he and Liz had their new baby. He did work on Little Austin for a while on the Sunday though and mentioned he had a surprise for them.

"I want to go for a walk," Helen said just as Rob was preparing for bed.

"In this? You must be kidding."

"Is it really so bad? I'm fed up with being stuck inside."

"I know you're restless, love but I don't think a late night stroll is a good idea. The local weather forecast said not to travel unless absolutely necessary."

"Yes of course it did. Sorry, I just can't seem to sit still. Staying in the same position seems to give me cramp and… ow!"

Her words were almost drowned out by a loud crash. Rob raced to the window and gasped.

"What's up?" Helen asked.

"Next door's tree has fallen onto our car."

"Little Austin?"

"No, the other one."

"That's OK then."

"No it isn't. We're going to need it soon."

"Why?"

"You're in labour."

He was right. Helen's contractions were mild and far apart, but the baby was definitely on the way.

Rob rang his dad to ask for a lift to the hospital. An hour later Dad called back.

"I'm sorry, I can't get through. They've closed off the roads due to floods. I tried Richie, but it's no better from his place. I'm not sure you'd be able to make it to St Anne's from yours either."

"Don't worry, Dad. I'll call a taxi," Rob said. "If they can't get us there, they'll take us somewhere else."

Rob tried, but they were all either stuck because of the flood or helping move evacuees.

"We can probably get someone to you in a couple of hours."

"I need someone quicker than that, my wife's having a baby."

"Better call an ambulance then."

Rob called, but of course they too were dealing with those affected by the flood. By the time Rob had given the details, Helen was screaming in pain. He held her hand and stroked her face, feeling totally helpless. Helen's breath was coming in sharp, shallow bursts and she was clammy with sweat. Every single person who'd expressed an opinion told them first babies always took time to be born. Every one of them was wrong… or maybe there was something wrong with Helen or the baby? If only he had one tenth of Great Aunt Mabel's knowledge and experience!

Wait a minute. He had her car and Richie had been working on it and said he had a surprise for them. Had he found and fitted that last engine piece?

"Helen love, there's a chance Richie's got Little Austin going."

The panic left her face. "Yes, yes! He'll get me to hospital. I'll be OK if I'm in Little Austin." Her breathing eased.

"Come on then."

Helen had to stop several times, on the walk to the garage, as another contraction gripped her, but she didn't scream, and looked stronger somehow. Rob helped her into the car then tried the engine. It started! He drove out, leaving the garage door wide open.

Little Austin's engine ran so smoothly it was as though the car was purring. Rob imagined he was happy to be out the garage at last and able to help his new owners. They stayed in a low gear to start, weaving between fallen branches, wheeled bins blown into the street and deep puddles.

As Rob turned onto the main road he said to Helen, "Amazing how different everything looks from a lower driving position."

"I suppose so, but everything seems different right now." She gripped his arm as another contraction gripped her.

Little Austin handled so well that Rob was able to keep the car on course despite that. Thankfully the wind had stopped by then and the rain wasn't much more than drizzle. The weather warning meant there were no other cars about, just as well as more of Rob's attention was on Helen than on the road. He actually got lost on the way to the hospital and travelled down a road he'd never seen before. Luck stayed with them though and that road led right up to the hospital. Rob ran inside and explained the situation.

Soon Helen and he were in a labour suite. Three hours later Helen gave birth to a six pound, two ounce son. Their baby boy was perfect, though Rob had to confirm that by touch as he couldn't see through his tears.

Rob was allowed to spend what remained of the night at the hospital. He was grateful as he was too tired to drive and certain he'd never again find the road he'd taken to get to the hospital and which seemed to be the only route which avoided the flood. In the morning he rang his father to give the family the good news.

"That's fantastic! Can I come over now?"

"If you like, but I think Helen's going to be let out fairly soon."

"I don't want to wait a moment longer than I have to to see my new grandson.

"So what are you calling him?" Dad asked once he'd counted all the fingers and toes.

"We haven't decided. It seemed like tempting fate to pick a name," Rob explained.

Helen grinned. He was sure she had something in mind and would tell him when she was ready. Rob hugged her and then gently touched his tiny, perfect son.

Dad said, "I heard on the radio that they've reopened most of the roads so I should be able to get you home OK."

"You?"

"They won't let you out of this place without a proper

baby seat in the car and I've got one fitted."

It wasn't until Dad was driving them back that Rob thought of what awaited them. Their car crushed under a tree and the garage doors left open and... he'd left Little Austin outside the hospital. How could he have forgotten that? It would have been clamped at the very least. He didn't say anything to Helen. Hopefully she was so absorbed by the baby he could sort everything out without worrying her.

Once Dad was gone and Helen and the baby were settled down for a nap, Rob went round to see his neighbour.

"I've called my insurers, taken photos and arranged for someone to come and remove the tree."

"Thank you," Rob said.

"Least I could do as it's my tree and you've got a baby on the way."

"Actually he was born last night."

"Congratulations! Did Helen have it at home then?"

"No, St Anne's."

"Oh. I thought the road was completely blocked." He pointed toward Rob's locked garage. "Suppose you'll be putting a baby seat in that funny little car of yours?"

"Definitely."

Rob checked the garage before going back indoors. Little Austin was safe and dry inside. Rob lifted the bonnet to inspect the shiny, but incomplete, engine. Odd. Just as odd as the fact that he'd found a road he didn't recognise which led to the hospital even though everyone said the route had been completely blocked last night. He couldn't understand it at all, but he perfectly understood and approved of Helen's name for their baby; Austin.

9. Vanished!

Maz was disappointed Maggie wasn't waiting at the bus stop. Over the last fortnight, Maz had worried about the old lady, but now something was obviously very wrong. She couldn't explain why, but she felt a connection to Maggie, almost as though anything bad that happened to Maggie might affect Maz.

Maz had first seen Maggie six months ago. Maz caught the 32 into town which got her to work just about on time. Maggie used the 17. Maz felt sorry for the old lady the first time she'd seen her, bundled up against the cold weather of early spring. How awful to be old and cold and alone.

Maggie was at the bus stop again the following day and the women had nodded an acknowledgement of each other, before checking they had their passes; a special pensioner's one in Maggie's case, an expensive monthly one in Maz's.

On the third day, Maggie had said, "It seems warmer this morning."

Maz turned the sound down on her i-Pod before asking for the remark to be repeated. Every morning of the following week, Maggie commented on the weather. Maz had agreed with her, but paid more attention to the text messages from her boyfriend, Robbie, than to the conversation.

The next week, Maggie had introduced herself. "My name is Maggie. Well, really it's Margaret, but everyone calls me Maggie."

"I'm Maz, but I was christened Margaret, too."

"What a coincidence! It's nice to feel we've got things in common."

Maz agreed, although she'd doubted they had much in common. Maz had a family she saw quite a bit of and a boyfriend she saw rather a lot of. Poor Maggie was probably all alone.

Her compassion for the old woman encouraged Maz to arrive earlier at the bus stop and spend longer chatting each morning. Now she glanced at her watch. The time dragged with nobody to talk to.

Maggie had been interested in everything Maz said. It seemed sad Maggie got her pleasure second-hand, so Maz had tried to remember any pleasant details.

"I heard a good story at work yesterday," she'd say whenever the joke was appropriate.

"I must remember that one," Maggie would say.

"Robbie took me to the pictures last night, we saw the new Hugh Grant film."

"Oooh, I like him," Maggie said. "I liked Cary Grant, too."

Maz nodded, wondering if Cary was Hugh's mother.

Thinking positively had a beneficial effect on Maz. Instead of remembering every tiny disappointment, she saw the bright side to each situation. She wanted Maggie to feel the same benefit. Maz never asked after the old lady's health as she was sure Maggie had aching joints and all manner of ills; it was better not to think of them. Maz didn't ask her new friend about her daily routine in case that revealed lonely days of endless boredom. The girl didn't enquire after friends and family who were surely long gone. Besides, it was easier to talk to Maggie than listen to her quiet words.

The two women had formed a vague kind of friendship.

"This is for you," Maggie had said one day, offering a carefully wrapped package. "It's chocolate cake; I made it yesterday."

"Thanks, I love home-made cake."

"I love baking them."

What a shame Maggie had nobody to cook for.

When Maz went on holiday, she brought back a gift for Maggie and told her about the lovely weather, food and scenery. She wasn't sure the old lady would approve of her travelling companion so didn't mention Robbie's lovely tan. He looked better than ever and Maz could hardly wait to see him that evening, so she could rub in after-sun lotion.

"…warm weather at our age."

Maz hadn't been paying attention, but nodded as though she'd heard.

Maggie passed on household tips, such as using newspaper for polishing windows and a way to stop bathroom mirrors steaming up. "Just dab on a little shaving foam and buff it off with a duster."

Maz had pulled out her earphones for that one, as applying make-up after her morning shower was always complicated by the constant need to wipe the mirror with her towel.

One day, Maz had been sending a text when Maggie arrived at the stop.

"Snap!" she said and held up a mobile. "It's just for emergencies, dear, but now I've got it, I'd like to know how it all works."

Maz had been pleased to show her friend how to use the phone. She hadn't needed to study the tiny print of the instructions as it was the same model as her own. She posed for a photo and set up a cheerful ringtone.

The last time Maz had seen Maggie, the old woman had said something about not being around and going to a better place. Before Maz could ask for the confusing statement to be repeated, the 32 arrived and she'd had to go. Maz thought no more of it until she realised Maggie had vanished.

The next morning Maggie hadn't been at the bus stop, but Maz assumed she'd been explaining her absence on the previous day. Maybe a doctor's appointment, or perhaps she was viewing some sheltered accommodation she was considering moving into; that would explain her reference to a better place. Maz hadn't worried until Maggie had been absent for three days. Even then she wasn't particularly concerned; perhaps Maggie just preferred to go out later or was shopping somewhere else – in a better place? Then Maz overheard a conversation on the bus about someone's neighbour who had died.

"She's in a better place now," the passenger had told her companion.

Was that what Maggie had meant? Did she know she was dying? Maz looked in the local paper to see if there was a notification of anyone called Margaret having died; there wasn't. Thinking back, she remembered Maggie had been very cheerful, excited even. Despite her sad lonely life, Maz didn't think she'd have been so cheerful about the thought of dying. Surely she wouldn't have broken the news in such a way? No, she must have been talking about something unconnected with her disappearance and since then, some incident had occurred.

Maz considered ringing round the hospitals, but she could hardly do that without knowing the patient's full name and when she'd been admitted. Two weeks passed with no sign of Maggie and no clue about her disappearance. If something bad could happen to a nice old lady like Maggie, it could happen to anyone.

Why hadn't she asked Maggie for her mobile number or offered hers in case of whatever emergency Maggie had bought the phone as protection against. Yes, Maz should definitely have done that. Poor old Maggie, alone and in need of help and her only friend had been too selfish to think of a way to provide it. The 17 arrived and Maz shook her head to indicate she wasn't waiting for it. As the bus pulled away, Maz blinked. The smoke must have got into her eyes, for a moment she thought she'd seen Maggie walking slowly towards her.

She looked again. A lady just like Maggie was approaching and she appeared to be carrying a huge straw donkey. Had the last fortnight all been some weird dream? Would Maz soon wake up ready to meet a perfectly safe Maggie at the bus stop? Whether illusion or real, Maggie was struggling with the donkey and Maz went to help her.

"Thank you so much, dear," Maggie said as she released her burden.

Maz pulled the speakers out of her ears; she was going to listen properly in future.

"Buying that for young Tom seemed such a good idea at the time, but I hadn't thought how I was going to get it onto the bus," Maggie continued. "I'm glad I got something smaller for you."

Maz unwrapped the package she was handed. It contained a very pretty string of beads.

"Thank you. Where did you go? I'm sorry, I didn't quite catch what you said the last time I saw you."

"I was saying that you wouldn't see me for a couple of

weeks as I was taking two weeks off work."

"Work?" Maz almost dropped the beads.

"Yes, I work in the DIY store on Newgate Lane; the same company you work for in town. My boyfriend and I have just been to the same resort in Spain that you visited. As the pair of us have so much in common, I knew I'd like the same place you enjoyed. Oh, there's your bus, dear. I'll see you tomorrow and you can tell me what you've been up to while I've been away."

"I think I'd rather listen to the details of your holiday, it sounds much more interesting," Maz said.

Maggie didn't seem to hear; her mobile was beeping.

"It's a text from my Bob to say he's taking our pictures to be developed. I'll show you them tomorrow – he looks ever so handsome with his tan."

Maz grinned as she boarded the bus. She had a feeling that looking at the pictures would be like looking into her own future – and she knew she'd like what she saw.

10. A Life Of Music

As a baby, Alwin received a tiny violin from his godfather. Arthur showed the growing boy how to hold it. Alwin played chords and scales before he could run across the park without falling. Learned tunes before he formed the letters of his own name. It came as naturally as sucking milkshake through a straw.

Aged ten, Alwin was described as a child genius. He played on the radio, even television a couple of times. He practised each day, performed every chance he got.

By his teens he was making more money each Saturday night than his father earned all week.

Then Alwin met Chloe. There had been other girls, but their smiles hadn't lifted and carried him the way a melody could. Their kisses hadn't vibrated through him like the echo of a song.

Arthur said, "There's a choice you must make, Alwin. Is the violin to be your whole life or just a part? You play well. You could be great, but it would require a great deal of work and sacrifice."

"What would you do?"

"You know what I did. I have a wife. I'm a happy man, but not a great musician."

Alwin thought over Arthur's words for days. Chloe was beautiful, sweet, and could make his heart ache. She haunted his thoughts like a tune. Perhaps the best tune he'd heard, would ever hear. She wasn't every note though. Not every chord and harmony.

Alwyn returned to Arthur. "I've decided on the music."

"Hold this." He handed Alwin a violin.

"I already have one."

"Hold it, think about it, then decide."

Alwin took the instrument. It was antique, very beautiful. He remembered hearing violins being described as a woman's body, a lover's body. He'd thought it was just because of the shape, but when he held that one he felt differently. "This is old. Special."

"It is. You'd have to commit to it completely. Like making a wedding vow…"

"Till death do us part?"

"No. More than that."

Alwin, looking into his godfather's eyes, knew he meant those words.

Alwin caressed the violin's long, slim neck. Allowed his fingers to trace the seductive curves of the bouts and waist. He and the violin could be great together if he gave his life to her.

"Yes," he whispered. It was like falling in love. He loved the instrument, the music. Without them he'd be miserable.

Arthur nodded his acceptance of the vow. "I know someone who can teach you."

"You're my teacher."

"I was, but you need more than me now."

"One of the sacrifices I have to make."

"I'm flattered you see it that way."

Never did Alwin neglect or abuse his darling. He lived for the music and for her. Gently holding her he practised for hours, showing his love with the passion of his playing. Not once did he over-tighten her strings, or forget to rosin the bow. Never did he torment her with an incorrect stance or poor technique.

Every standing ovation, each recording deal was gracefully accepted as a tribute to his love. There were many such tributes.

Alwin aged in a way his violin never could. He couldn't stand so long. His elbow sank during performances. Joints creaked and muscles ached. She helped him. As the notes left her they reverberated through his body, giving him strength. She carried him through faultlessly until his bow was still and only the echo of their music remained.

A nurse placed the violin on his chest as Alwin lay dying. His arms didn't have the strength to hold his love in the correct position. Nor lift a bow or pluck the strings, but as he cradled her in his arms she whispered to him. Faintly at first, the beautiful music they'd made together reached him. It swelled and filled him.

The stiffness is gone from his fingers now. Alwin can play for hours and never flag. His limbs are strong. He stands tall and moves forward, his steps as light as though he's dancing. Her arms wrap around him. He feels the warmth of her skin under his fingers and the beat of her heart against his chest. They'll be together for eternity now, playing an endless symphony of love.

11. Waiting For A Friend

Truda sipped her tea and looked out onto the street. Living at the end of a quiet cul-de-sac meant there was little to see, but sometimes there were children playing, or being taught to ride bicycles. It was a favourite spot for practising three-point turns too. People rarely passed by, and at eighty-two she'd outlived her friends, but Truda still had regular visitors, especially in bad weather. Kindly neighbours offered to fetch shopping or shovel snow from her path.

Oh, there was Sarah, from next door. How nice of her to call. Truda let her in.

"Hi, Truda. I've got a favour to ask."

"How can I help?" She'd be delighted to assist Sarah. She often called round to see that Truda was OK or took her to the supermarket, and held a door key 'just in case'. She also spared the time to drink tea and chat with Truda about once a week. Truda didn't like to suggest it more often than that for fear of being a nuisance. Young people all had such busy lives. Truda and her friends had been just the same.

"Thing is, they've done up Solent House into fancy retirement flats. You know, the place off Bridge Street?"

Truda nodded to say she was aware of the building. She didn't say how well she knew it.

"It's been derelict for absolutely ages and I'd love to see what they've done. Will you come with me and look?"

"If you'd like me to." For the first time ever, Truda was reluctant to accept an invitation from her neighbour. These days memories were her companions and naturally she preferred the pleasant ones.

As they drove to Bridge Street, Sarah revealed the reason behind her interest. "When I was a kid I went in there. I didn't break in exactly, just climbed in through a window which wasn't very secure. I didn't stay long as I convinced myself it was haunted. Long enough to see it had been grand once though and I'd be interested to see how it looks now."

"What made you think it was haunted?"

"There was a girl in one room. Well sort of there and not there. She seemed to be sitting on a chair, but there wasn't any furniture. Of course there was no girl either, I just imagined her and what she said."

"Oh?" Truda barely whispered the word, but it was enough to prompt Sarah.

"She said she was really lonely and asked me to stay and talk. I just ran. A few days later I persuaded a friend to go back with me, but the windows were all boarded up by then and we couldn't get in."

Truda didn't have long to wonder if that memory had anything to do with Sarah's kindness to her, as they were soon at Solent House. A large sign stated 'just one apartment remaining'.

"That's just a sales gimmick I reckon," Sarah said. "That sign has been up at least a week."

They walked through the attractive gardens and approached the magnificent old building.

"They've done a good job. It's just as I remember it," Truda said.

"You've been here before?"

"A very long time ago."

"And was it… Were there any rumours it was…"

"Haunted? No. There were no ghosts then." There had been a little girl. "Rebecca," Truda whispered.

"Pardon?"

"Sorry, I was just remembering something. Let's go in and look round."

At first it seemed to Truda the downstairs hadn't changed at all. Double glazing and other improvements had been made without spoiling the house. As they looked round it became clear many large rooms had been divided up and of course the scullery and kitchen with the huge wood fired range were long gone.

One beautiful reception room had been kept intact as a communal lounge and it was there a saleswoman was explaining to someone else that she was sorry, but the only residence still available was the one they'd just viewed.

The potential customer was clearly disappointed.

"Maybe I was wrong about the sales gimmick," Sarah said.

Truda asked to see the flat.

"Certainly, if you'd like to follow me."

"If they've sold all but one, there must be something wrong with this one," Sarah whispered. They stepped out the lift behind the saleswoman, ignoring her rehearsed speech about the advantages of life at Solent House.

The saleswoman stopped in the corridor and held open the door to allow them to enter. Sarah gasped and hung back as Truda stepped inside. She needed only a moment to see Sarah's reaction wasn't because of any fault in the room. It was really lovely. Did the young woman recognise it as the one in which she'd thought she'd seen a ghost, or could she actually see Rebecca and hear her invitation to stay and talk?

"Would you mind if I looked around on my own?" Truda asked.

After the other two had hurried away, Truda dragged one chair over to the ghost and positioned it under her seated form, then sat in the other. "Have you been here all this time, Rebecca?"

"I was born here. I died here and it seems I'll be here forever. In all that time I've only had one friend. Oh! You called me by my name. You know me?"

Rebecca was the spoilt daughter of Solent House's wealthy owners and Truda was the child of their cook. Truda could have been jealous, but instead she felt sorry for the girl who had no friends because none of the local children were considered good enough for her to associate with. Whenever she could do it without getting them both into trouble, Truda would talk to the other girl and even play games when her parents were out.

When Rebecca developed scarlet fever she was nursed in the house. She was kept isolated for fear she'd pass on the infection. Not even her parents were permitted close to their daughter. Truda had sat beneath her window, reading stories to her friend who was too weak to call a response.

"It's you isn't it, Truda? You've come back. Will you stay?"

"Yes, yes I think I will if I'll have you for company."

"Of course you will. I've always known I'd stayed here for a reason and now I see that it was to be reunited with my friend. When we leave here it will be together, but that's not going to be for a while yet."

When Sarah and the saleswoman returned they brought tea for Truda. They both seemed surprised with her intention to take the flat. The saleswoman was of course delighted and left again to fetch the necessary paperwork.

"Are you sure this is what you want?" Sarah asked. "I feel sort of responsible as it was my idea to come here and well, this room…"

"It's the one you were in before?"

"Yes. I can't see anything now, but there's a kind of feeling."

"I have a feeling too." As Truda sipped her tea she looked out onto the street. From her new flat there was quite a lot to see and now she'd have someone to share it all with. "I feel I shall be very happy here."

12. Etched On The Heart

I didn't notice the brass plaque the first few times I sat on the bench. I had other things on my mind; Troy had left the week before. Already I hated that he wouldn't be there waiting when I returned from my walk. I'd received text messages from him for the first couple of days, checking I was OK, but it was no surprise they'd soon stopped.

Climbing Beacon Hill was a ritual I'd begun the day Troy left. Hills are good places to get things in perspective. Looking down on the town where I lived reminded me how small I was and somehow that made my concerns seem a little smaller too. It turned them from big worries into mental puzzles I could solve if I tried.

Solving problems is something I'm good at. So good I have my own one-woman accountancy business. Being self-employed is great in a lot of ways. I can plan my day, take time off when the weather is nice and avoid the roads when they're busy. There are dangers too. As I'm the only one who always knows where I am and what I'm doing, I could easily sneak home to watch daytime TV or worse.

Without Troy to entice me away from the spreadsheets to socialise and get some exercise I was actually more at risk from overwork. There was a strong temptation to throw myself into the job and hope it would blot out everything else. That's why I started the walks. The hill is steep enough to get my heart pumping faster than usual, but not so challenging I can't make time, or need a shower afterwards.

The bench was the obvious place to aim for and I must have used it at least four times before I saw the plaque. It was shiny and new looking, so perhaps it hadn't been there earlier? 'In memory of Bob and Bertie, who loved this spot' was etched into it in neat, crisp letters. That suggested two men, but then my own name of Bailey is sometimes assumed to be male by people who see it written down, so I've learned not to jump to conclusions about that kind of thing.

Perhaps one of them was really a Roberta? They could both be women for all I knew, but I didn't think so. As I ran my fingers over the engraved plaque, I was sure they weren't. Whoever they were, they must be dead. The 'in memory' part wouldn't be there otherwise. No dates were given. Did they die one soon after the other? Were they a couple, war comrades, siblings?

I liked the mystery; it gave me something to think about other than Troy's proposal. He's in the navy, away on his ship. He'd hoped we'd be engaged by the time he sailed, but I said I needed time to think. That's not selfish is it, to want to be sure before committing myself?

As his ship sailed out of UK waters the phone signal was lost and he sent emails rather than texts. I preferred those as I could almost hear his voice when I read them. He seemed his usual optimistic self. No hint of a sulk because I didn't give him the answer he wanted.

Troy told me how he was settling in, what his crew mates were like. I told him about my walks and Bob and Bertie's plaque.

'Maybe one day there'll be a bench with a plaque dedicated to Troy and Bailey?' he suggested, making it clear he'd not given up.

'Maybe,' I typed back, letting him know that I was still thinking. It wasn't that I didn't love him or doubted his love for me, but would that be enough? His career in the navy was only just beginning. He'd be away often for months at a time. There would be temptations.

I took those thoughts up Beacon Hill and sat with them on the bench at the top. As had become my habit I ran a finger over the plaque. The answer came to me. Dogs! Bertie and Bob were dogs. I could picture them easily. Bob was a small black one, some kind of terrier possibly, I'm not good on dog breeds. Bertie was a bigger brown one. Guide dog kind of size, but lankier than that, with quite big floppy ears and a white patch over one eye.

As I moved my hand from the plaque the image faded. I was sure I was right though. Although I still didn't know how to answer Troy, I walked back down the hill and set off to visit my next client with a smile on my face.

When I reached the bench the following day, there was an elderly man resting there. As a change from the view, I tactfully studied him as I circled the top of the hill. He touched the plaque and talked to no one. No, that's not quite right. I couldn't see anyone, but I thought maybe he could. The dogs? Maybe they were his and now he walked without them.

The man became a regular visitor. Or perhaps he always had been and, like with the plaque, I just hadn't noticed him at first. Often I saw him as I walked up or down or he'd be sitting on the bench when I reached the top. I nodded as we passed each other and he returned the acknowledgement, but we never spoke.

On my next visits, whenever the bench was unoccupied, I placed my hand on the plaque and imagined the dogs playing together. Sometimes I saw them as pups, sometimes as older dogs. They scampered around, tumbling over each other, or wandering off to sniff a tuft of grass. They never went far and always, just before the mental image faded, they'd sit and wait. I never saw an imaginary owner throw them a stick, call them to heel, or offer a treat. They either amused themselves, or waited.

One day I sensed there was something different about the old man. It was the first time I'd seen him in the evening and I felt he'd been there some time. There was something different about the way he was talking too. I did a circuit of the top of the hill and saw him get up and walk away. When I got back to the bench I spotted a pale peach rose and knew he'd left it there.

I soon knew who he'd left it for. There was another plaque for her, next to Bertie and Bob's and engraved in the same style. Her name was Florence and her birth and death dates were given on the top half of the new brass plaque. She'd died just a few days before and if my maths were right, which they certainly should be, she was ninety-two.

When I touched the plaque I saw her. Young and pretty, dancing. Older, baking. Holding a child. Young again in a wedding dress, then older with the dogs. After the series of fleeting images I felt her waiting.

And I waited for Troy. There were temptations, or there could have been. I frequently visited clients and their employees, many of them young and single. I saw walkers and joggers on the hill as I walked and knew some noticed me. Men in the supermarket glanced from my face and figure to the basket of food for one. I could easily have repeated my earlier mistake. I cheated on a previous boyfriend. We were young and it wasn't a really serious relationship, or so I excused myself. I'd been on a training course. Let's just say my boss could have saved some money by not bothering to book my hotel room.

I knew Troy would often be away from me. I could easily do the same thing again and quite likely I'd get away with it. It wasn't going to happen again. As I sat on the bench I knew I wouldn't do that to Troy. I loved him too much.

I considered waiting until he came home to tell him I'd made up my mind, so I could see the joy on his face, but that would leave him with another month of uncertainty. I emailed as soon as I got in and felt his joy as I read the reply a few hours later.

I didn't climb Beacon Hill for a while after that. It rained. Work was busy. I jogged sometimes and chose to run on the flat. There were all kinds of reasons, but the main one was that I didn't need to. I'd been drawn up there, to clear my head in the breeze, to contemplate the view, to make up my mind to marry Troy – and I'd done that.

When he came home, that look of delight I thought I'd missed appeared on his face when he saw me. We were soon busy with wedding plans as we didn't have long to get everything organised in time for a honeymoon before he went away again.

"What finally convinced you?" Troy asked.

I told him about the walks and the bench and how it had seemed to help me see things clearly. When at last we had the time for a walk we climbed Beacon Hill together and sat on the bench.

We noticed the space under Florence's name and dates had been filled in. Her husband had not outlived her long. I touched his name and for a moment thought I could see him. No longer old and bent, he strode towards her with another peach coloured rose in his hand. She ran towards him, arms outstretched as though they were in a romantic film. That's probably where the images had come from – a film I'd seen once and forgotten until something about the hill or the view triggered a memory. He picked her up and swung her around. The two dogs raced about, yapping excitedly and literally jumping with joy.

I smiled at the image as it faded, happy in the knowledge that their waiting had been worthwhile and was over. A bit like Troy and me. There would be times we'd be apart, but I'd wait and when he left the navy and we were together permanently it would have been worth it and we'd spend the rest of our lives together. Who knows, maybe even death won't separate us.

I turned to Troy, wanting to share some of that with him. His eyes were closed and there was a smile on his face, as though he were watching a scene as happy as the one I'd just imagined. I placed my hand over his, where it rested against Bertie and Bob's plaque.

"That was weird," Troy said. "Sort of like a dream. I was just wondering who Bertie and Bob might be and then I seemed to see them. Two little boys. One small with dark hair and a bigger, lanky brown haired one. They were waiting for their dad to come home."

He reached for my other hand. "Bailey, we've never properly talked about having children. I've just sort of assumed we would… is it something you want?"

"Yes, definitely. Besides, in seventy years or so we're going to need someone to come up here and fix our plaque to the bench, aren't we?"

"We will. Now we'd better get back down and talk to the florist. I want to order peach roses for the men's buttonholes to match the ones you've picked out for your bouquet."

13. Disbelieving Des

I'm running along behind my mates, screaming just like them, when I remember I don't believe in ghosts. The screaming part I pack in straight away. Feel pretty ashamed of myself for starting it really. I'm fifteen, not six, and although I'm female I've never been one for acting all stupid and girlie. Well, maybe around Craig in the lower sixth, but that's different. Spiders don't scare me and I won't wear clothes I hate just because they're fashionable. I'm not totally gullible you see. Unlike Mum.

Takes me a bit longer to stop rushing after Sheila and Roz. Just because there's no such thing as ghosts doesn't mean I want to be out in the dark in a strange place on my own. Tell the truth it is sort of creepy and I feel kind of lightheaded. Maybe all that running and screaming starved my brain of oxygen.

Where am I anyway? Nothing, except for my mates up ahead, looks familiar. I don't believe I've been here before. That phrase again! Mum said it'd get me into trouble.

My reply had been, "I don't believe you."

"Destiny, love, you have to have faith." Then she told me all over again about the old woman she'd helped once, who gave her a locket to give to her daughter, which would give that daughter a second chance, but only if she truly believed. Blah, blah, blah. This happened back when Mum was thirty-eight and thought she'd never have a baby. I was born just before she turned forty. She thinks it was a miracle. I think it's just an excuse for giving me a rubbish name.

Something tells me she could be right this time. Not with all that fate stuff, I don't mean, but with me getting into trouble because of not believing. There's loads of stuff I don't believe in. Ghosts, God, that Craig in the lower sixth will ever ask me out, fairies, UFOs, crusts make your hair curl. My mates all call me Disbelieving Des because of it. That might be why I'm here, I can half remember a connection…

Think back, Destiny. What's the last thing I do remember? Oh yeah. Getting told off for not doing my maths homework. Come on, it was algebra! What. is. the. actual. point?

"Destiny Partington, your homework please," old Add-em-Up Adams asked, after flipping through the pile of paperwork on his desk.

"I haven't done it, sir."

"And why is that, Miss Partington?"

"I don't believe in it, sir."

He'd come over, put his hands on my desk and leant forward a bit. Reckon everyone else in the class was leaning forward as well. They'd gone dead quiet, waiting to see what would happen.

Add-em-Up smiled. "I believe that you're in detention, young lady."

Everyone laughed, even my so called besties, Roz and Sheila.

That's it! It's all coming back in a rush now. We were going over to Seagull's Cry. Them to look for ghosts, me to laugh at them for being so daft. Because of my detention, we'd met up at the ruined house later than planned.

They wouldn't go upstairs because of it being haunted and I'd gone on my own. Then... something... then we were all running out screaming. I fell! Of course. Must have banged my head which is why I feel so odd.

I was lying on the ground looking at the doorway. There was lots of yelling and then the others came running in. I could only see their feet, so I tried to move my head, but it just flopped over to the other side, giving me a close up view of a manky skirting board.

"Her neck... what's wrong with her neck?" Roz asked.

"Dunno, but I'm calling an ambulance." That was Sheila.

"Shall we move all the stuff off her?"

"Better not. We might make things worse."

"Worse than a broken neck?"

By then I was wondering what stuff was on me. I tried to push against it and found myself standing on my feet. They screamed and ran out the back. It took me longer, but I followed. That's why I don't recognise anything, I've never been round the back of the house before.

I return to the house. Footsteps follow. The others must have realised how stupid they were being and come back to check I'm OK. But I'm not! That's me on the floor. Broken neck, huge pile of rotten wood on top of her... Everything is grey and dusty. Her clothes. Her skin, hair. Mine. Me.

There's something gleaming in amongst the dust. My locket. Inside, so I've always been told, is my second chance. That doesn't sound likely until I consider the alternative; that my body is lying dead on the floor and I'm a ghost. Can't be; I don't believe in ghosts.

Second chances? Add-em-Up let me do my homework during detention and he explained those equations all over again. I understand them now. Then on the way out of school I heard someone call my name. It was Craig, he'd been at Rugby practice.

"Fancy going for a burger?" he'd asked.

"Yeah, but not today. I'm meeting my mates."

We arranged it for Saturday, but I can't go if I'm dead. Oh yes, I believe in second chances. Truly believe.

There's lots of yelling and then my friends come running in. I can only see their feet, so I try to move my head. Nothing happens.

"Her neck… what's wrong with her neck?" Roz asks.

"Dunno, but I'm calling an ambulance." That's Sheila.

"It's her locket. I think it's strangling her."

I feel fingers at my neck, then air rushing into my lungs. Not much as there's the weight of rotten floorboards pressing down on my chest, but I'm breathing.

"Oh no! I've broken it open," Roz says. "You know how she gets if anyone even mentions looking inside."

Sheila replies, "She'll forgive you under the circumstances. Look, she's getting some colour back. I think she'll be OK."

You know what, I believe she's right.

14. Predictions At The Pictures

I wish I'd known about Liz's sixth sense before my job interview. I wouldn't have been so nervous then. She was the one who'd let me in and taken me to the manager's office. We'd chatted on the way.

"I look forward to working with you," she said after knocking on the door. She knew, or guessed I suppose you'd say if you're as sceptical as I was then, that I'd get the job.

Although she was right, I didn't immediately think much of her predicting that we'd work together. My friends say I'm gullible, but it's not true.

In the local cinema, that's where our jobs are, mine and Liz's and five others. I sell tickets and ice creams, or show people to seats or even vacuum the floors. Might not sound like much, but jobs are few and far between around here and there are perks. I can watch any films I like for free when I'm not working and bring friends and family as long as it's not too many of them or too often. Nice place it is. Still owned by the same family who opened it back in the '30s.

It's art deco apparently. Some people come to see the building more than the films. Sometimes they want to do that when there's nothing showing and take pictures. Boss said they can do as they like as long as they pay to come in and don't spill nothing on the seats.

"We ask Liz if they're likely to make a mess," one of the others said and a few of them laughed.

Liz always said they wouldn't. They didn't, but there's not

much in that. Photographing and making notes about the staircase handrail and the tiles in the lav seems weird to me, but the people doing it were always tidy.

Once, as I was going home, Liz suggested I borrow an umbrella from lost property. I didn't take much notice; there was hardly a cloud in the sky. It didn't rain but the council were cleaning graffiti off a wall. If I'd had a brolly I could have dashed by without getting soaked by spray from the high pressure water jets. As it was I had to go home the long way and had blisters on my heels before I was there. When she suggested the same thing after that I always took one; and always ended up using it. I wasn't the only one who took her advice, but the others claimed it was because they'd heard the weather forecast.

One day, not long after I'd started, the film being shown was a romance. A couple came in, well lots of couples obviously, but Liz pointed out this particular pair and said they weren't married. Least ways not to each other. The other girls rolled their eyes. "Here she goes again." They waved their fingers in what I suppose was supposed to be a witchy kind of way and said, "It's a sign."

"There's a sci-fi next week, she'll probably point out some strange looking customer and say he's an alien."

"Don't be daft," Liz said. "It's not a sign of anything, I'm just saying they're not married is all."

I hoped she was wrong in her assumption the couple were up to no good. I'm a romantic and he looked charming. Tall, dark and handsome; the works. Not that he'd have looked at little mousey me but I wanted to believe there were women out there happily settled with just such a man. It somehow would make my own chances seem better. She was right though, Liz. He came back two days later with a different woman. He looked more smarmy than charming the second time.

One of the girls announced she was pregnant. There was a lot of excited congratulations, but one or two people seemed especially pleased that Liz, with her special powers, hadn't guessed.

"Guessed what?" Liz asked, coming in at the end of this.

"I'm pregnant."

"You didn't guess, Liz, so she won't be naming it after you!"

"No, neither boy would thank you for calling him Elizabeth."

They laughed then, pleased she'd taken their teasing so well.

When the sci-fi film ran, Liz didn't suggest any of the clients were from another planet, but I did see one who seemed out of this world. Not so obviously good looking as the love cheat I suppose, but there was something about him which appealed to me. See, I don't learn! Or to put a more positive spin on it, I don't let one little setback put me off. There was no romance up on the screen, but that didn't mean I couldn't daydream about starring in my own, did it?

Liz hadn't learned to keep her observations to herself though and said, "That young man is going to lose something."

That set the others off with their gypsy impressions again. Still she was proved right when he came back the next night for his dropped pen. Luckily I got to speak to him and asked him to fill in one of the lost property claim forms. Usually we wouldn't bother for a plain biro, they're for in case there's a dispute over something valuable, but I got him to do it so's I'd know his name. It's Gary Venables. I got to know his phone number and address too, but made a point of not remembering them so I wasn't tempted to hang about where he lived in case I bumped in to him.

But then I thought what happens if I do go there for some reason and do bump into him accidentally? It would look as though I'd done it on purpose and was stalking him so I had to look it up and then not go there. My friends say that sometimes I overthink things. Guess they're right. He lived somewhere I don't usually go, so it was OK.

Gary came back again with a kid. His nephew he told me, so that was OK too. I guessed he'd watched the film himself first to make sure it was all right to take the lad. Man like that would make a good father, I thought.

Talking of children, the mother-to-be who said she wouldn't name her baby after Liz came in two days later to say she'd had a scan and really was expecting twins. Twin boys it was believed.

The next film we showed was a thriller. There's only the one screen so we run one for a week or so and then have a change, or sometimes it's a kids one early and then another afterwards. All depends. My friends say I get sidetracked. Guess they're right about that too. Anyway there was a thriller on. First showing and a Saturday night so it was busy. Hardly had a chance to speak but once Liz said, "Those two are up to no good."

I had a quick look to see who she meant, but everything seemed OK to me.

"Should I call the boss down?" I asked her. If there's any trouble, which there hardly ever is, we're supposed to let him know.

"No, just a feeling I had."

Seemed to me she had pointed to the group of three men

I'd sold tickets to. They'd seemed OK, maybe they'd been drinking but they were quiet with it so I hadn't been bothered. The queue was getting impatient so I just got on with my job.

Liz's words were forgotten in the excitement which followed the film. No, not excitement. You'd think a dead body would cause some, but it didn't. A dull kind of shock was more like it. Most of the public had left and a few of us ushered the rest out while someone called an ambulance, even though it seemed unlikely they could do anything. Liz said they couldn't anyway.

I suppose someone else got hold of the boss and he called the police. They soon arrived and the ambulance people. The body was taken out in one of those black bags like you see on the news. Horrible it was. Not even the sight of Gary Venables cheered me up. Well it might have done if it hadn't turned out he was a police detective. I don't mean I don't like the police, but you see he said he thought the man had been murdered. That wasn't cheery. We all had to give statements. Gary was nice about it and so were the other police but it's all a bit of a blur to be honest.

Don't know how word got around, but once we were able to open up again we were busier than ever. The boss changed the cover on one of the seats for a brand new one in a different colour. It's not the one where the murdered man had been sitting, just one which got chewing gum on once and the stuff it was removed with had spoiled the finish, but we sold more seats in that area than elsewhere. Not the actual seat, but those next to and behind it. People are odd aren't they?

The girls had all kinds of theories about who the man was and why he'd been killed and who'd done it. A few people reckoned it was a spy kind of deal. They'd realised, right after he told us, Gary was a policeman. They knew he'd been into the cinema several times and reckoned he'd been staking it out. Liz didn't think so. I was glad. I didn't like the thought of him being involved in anything dangerous. I did like the idea of him investigating the case though, at least if it involved him spending more time at the scene of the crime.

"Do you think spending time here will help him get his man?" I asked Liz.

"No, but it might help him get his woman."

"You think the killer was a woman? Who?" the others started asking.

Liz winked at me before pointing out they didn't believe in her feelings about things. I did by then, she sees things other people don't, but somehow I didn't think she'd been talking about the murder.

"Come on, Liz, who do you think did it?" my colleagues coaxed.

As they gently teased her she said, "Maybe it was aliens?" I remembered her remarks about the three men. To be honest, I didn't think that had any bearing on the case, but Gary had asked us to contact him if we remembered anything at all, however trivial it might seem, and I did want to contact him. He has a lovely voice. He said he'd come right over, which was even better than having him at the end of the phone.

Now I don't have Liz's sixth sense, but I got the distinct impression he was making a lot more of this potential lead than he truly thought it deserved. First off he asked the boss if he could see the CCTV footage from that night, once again, and then he insisted I watch it with him. I felt a bit of an idiot when I realised that of course they'd already checked it, still it was nice to sit with him.

"There, that's them," I said when I recognised the three Liz had drawn my attention to.

We watched carefully and noticed that two of the men kept hold of the other and one or other of them was always between his face and me and that they, or at least an arm was always obscuring his face from the security cameras.

"I think maybe your friend was right," Gary said. "We paid more attention to the cameras in the auditorium and when people left, but this does look suspicious."

The tape was shown to other police forces and soon another officer recognised the men and the crime was solved. A falling out over drugs money apparently, the victim as bad as his killers. But I'm not telling his story, I'm telling mine. Mine and Gary's. You see Liz was right and he did get his woman; me. She'd been right long before that though. I know because I asked him if he'd really been staking out the cinema.

"In a way. You see the first time I came here I lost something."

He had, just as Liz had said he would. "Your pen."

He shook his head. "I dropped it deliberately as an excuse to come back and speak to you. What I'd really lost was my heart."

"We could all see it coming," the others said when I told them we were seeing each other. I don't believe them. Like I said I'm not completely gullible.

15. Lucille

Gloria hated the idea of driving a car in which someone had died. She wished Nathan hadn't told her. She wished she didn't need a car at all. It had been a surprise when, after losing his own licence, Nathan insisted she learn to drive.

Nathan begrudged giving her the money for lessons. He'd reluctantly agreed after she pointed out she could only afford one a fortnight on her wages. That meant it would be months before she was ready for the test.

"You'll take an intensive course and pass quickly."

"I can't do that… my job."

"You'll have to pack that in anyway, once you're driving me around."

Gloria nearly cried. She'd only begun working since she'd turned thirty-eight and the twins started college. It was part-time, as Nathan demanded a proper breakfast before work and to come home to a spotless house, his dinner on the table and tomorrow's shirt perfectly ironed. Her four hours away from home with friendly conversation and praise for a job well done were pure joy. She'd guessed she wouldn't be staying long, but thought she'd have a few months. It was Nathan who'd drunk before driving, but she who must pay the price, although he did have to write cheques for her driving course and tests.

The kind, patient instructor made her feel capable and confident. She passed first time. Nathan didn't congratulate her. He ordered her onto a bus with him, to collect the car he'd bought. Gloria felt she should have been consulted, but didn't dare complain. Angry scenes at home were bad enough, she couldn't face one on public transport. Instead, she asked about the make. It was the same as the one in which she'd taken her test. Foolishly, Gloria smiled at that and was instantly punished.

"The previous lady owner died in the driver's seat," Nathan told her.

Gloria decided naming the car might make it seem less intimidating. The moment she saw it, the name Lucille sprang to mind. Until then she'd dreaded driving home with Nathan beside her, but she stopped worrying. She'd easily passed her test and if Nathan expected to be driven around then he must accept his wife was a capable driver. Gloria felt a warm glow as she realised the balance of power in their relationship had tipped, not exactly into her favour, but not quite so far out of it. Immediately she was saddened, what a way to consider a marriage; surely it should be a partnership not a fight? Maybe spending time side by side in the small car would bring them emotionally closer. She hoped so.

Gloria drove Nathan to appointments, waited in Lucille and took him to the next meeting. At home, he'd watch critically the preparations for their evening meal, glancing frequently at his watch. As she served, he sat, waiting for her to bring in both meals and return to the kitchen for his beer. After supper, she did the housework, using the vacuum only during the advertisements. Then she washed and ironed his clothes and polished his shoes. When he was in bed, she cleaned the bathroom ready for the morning. Soon, she was tired.

"How can you be? You don't work at all now. I hope you aren't going to be ill, I have important meetings coming up."

The next day Nathan came out of a building and stood on the pavement, impatiently awaiting collection. To reach him, Gloria would need to force her way on to the congested main road, negotiate a busy junction then tackle the one way system across town, until finally she was back almost where she'd started. If Nathan would just use the subway, they could simply leave by the car park's other exit and be on their way, with no need to break the speed limit in order to be on time for the next appointment.

The car wouldn't start. She tried several times, but there was nothing. Lucille had fuel. The lights and radio worked, so there was no problem with the battery. She opened the bonnet, but could see nothing obviously wrong.

"What are you messing about at?" Nathan demanded. "You should be watching out for me, not poking about in there. If anyone had seen me waving to you and being ignored, I'd have looked very unprofessional. As it was, I had the presence of mind to use the subway. You'll have to get this suit cleaned now, you know how those places smell."

Gloria hadn't noticed a smell, but kept quiet and turned the key again. The car started.

Later that morning, whilst waiting for Nathan, Gloria spotted a young man staring at her. He was extremely pale and looked as though he might faint. Gloria cautiously wound down her window and asked if he was OK.

"Sorry, that was my mother's car, it was a shock to see it."

Gloria insisted he join her for a cup of tea. He wouldn't allow her to buy a drink, but said he welcomed the chance to sit and chat while she drank hers. When he spoke about his mother, he seemed no more than a child. His dad had been a bully, he told her. As his mother never complained, no one realised how unhappy she was.

"She used to go for long drives in the car to get away from him. The day she died, she'd said she didn't feel well and needed to go to hospital. He took no notice and she got into the car to drive herself. She didn't get far before she pulled over. After five hours he wondered where she was, and found her dead at the wheel."

"I'm so sorry," Gloria said.

The young man shrugged.

"I'm glad you've got the car now. Mother loved driving, it allowed her to escape him and visit me each week. Mum would be pleased to know it's being used as something other than a means of escape."

Gloria couldn't tell him that driving the car prevented her own means of escape. Instead she pretended she visited her children and went to gardens.

"Mother loved flowers; she used to bring them to me."

"It sounds as though you were very close."

"Oh yes, she told me everything."

"That must have been a great comfort to her."

He left, seeming happier.

Gloria returned to the car as Nathan left the building opposite. Two hours she'd waited, at least today, she'd had a chat and a cup of tea, usually her time was completely wasted. It would be a good idea to bring a book.

She wondered if her words to the young man could become true? A quick check of her map, as Nathan waited at the crossing, revealed that his next appointment was near a public garden. She could drop him off, look round and collect him later. Gloria wouldn't allow herself to become the second owner of Lucille to be bullied into unhappiness.

After reaching the correct street and searching for a parking space, she asked how long he'd be.

"As long as it takes."

"Nathan, you must know how long you are likely to be."

"What difference does it make; you'll have to wait however long I am. Unless you've got something better to do."

"I thought I'd go and look at a garden."

"And that's more important than ensuring I reach my next appointment? You must have forgotten who makes the money for your food and the roof over your head."

"No, I haven't forgotten. I'll be here to collect you right on time, if you can just bring yourself to tell me what that time is."

"Why, you cheeky..." Nathan screeched.

"No, Nathan, don't yell at me," Gloria shouted, surprising them both. "As you can't decide how long you'll be, I'll be back in an hour and a half. Now get going, or you'll be late."

"I don't know what's got into you," he said, although with less anger than he frequently used toward her.

Gloria didn't know either. She was shaking as she locked Lucille outside the garden. The quiet green space comforted her. She walked for half an hour enjoying the scent of the flowers and the feel of soft grass under her feet, before sitting on a bench in a sunny spot. The warmth and scent of the flowers reminded her of another park. Gloria and Nathan used to eat their lunch together whenever it had been sunny. There had been a lot of sunny days and sometimes they'd wandered away from the crowds in search of shade. Hand in hand, they'd sought out a private spot to kiss and cuddle. In the evenings they'd rush home to finish what they'd started in the lunch break.

A giggle interrupted her thoughts. Gloria opened her eyes to see a young couple sprawled on the grass. The boy was slowly stroking suntan lotion over the girl's bare shoulders. Nathan used to do that to her. It was all so long ago. These days if he'd ever found himself sat in the sun with her, rather than concocting excuses to stroke her skin, he'd be snapping at her to cover herself up.

Nathan was waiting by the car when she returned. He got in without a word.

It seemed his sullen mood and her own irritation were summoning the heavy clouds which darkened the sky. The rain was heavy by the time she dropped Nathan off for his last appointment.

"Make sure you're back here by five-thirty; the place shuts then and I don't want to stand in the rain waiting for you."

The rain eased soon after, but the roads were slick, the ground saturated. Gloria decided it wasn't a good time to explore. At five, she began driving slowly past the building, glancing into the lobby on each occasion, hoping Nathan would be finished and they could go home. He didn't appear until exactly half past. Gloria drove up and gently applied the brake. Lucille kept going, splashing through a puddle. Greasy water splashed Nathan. She braked again and the car stopped fifty yards ahead of Nathan.

He wrenched open the door. "What are you playing at? Look at my suit."

Gloria looked. "Oh yes, you were right, it does need cleaning."

On Saturday, Gloria borrowed a book from the library and looked up free entry gardens near Nathan's business appointments. She visited several over the next few days. When there was nowhere convenient, she read a book. She finished reading the chapter before starting the car and taking Nathan to his next destination. Somehow having the car gave her courage. Gloria told him about the places she'd visited so they didn't sit in stony silence. He pretended to be asleep in bed to avoid acknowledging her, but he couldn't do that in the car. Occasionally he forgot to communicate only in grunts and they had a proper conversation.

She refused to drive Nathan to the pub, or collect alcohol for him when doing the shopping. Having to walk to the off-licence and carry his beer home dramatically reduced his intake. Without the beer, he was a nicer person.

Gloria decided to visit their children.

"I don't want to go," Nathan informed her.

"Then don't. I'm sure I can manage for a day without you."

"A day? What am I supposed to do for lunch?"

"I don't know, Nathan, but I expect you'll think of something."

Her day with the twins was a success. They weren't very surprised to learn their father had lost his licence; they were amazed their mother had gained one. It was the first time she'd really talked to them since they were tiny. Gloria suspected they'd been surprised to learn their mother had a personality. They had another surprise to come, but she wasn't ready to share it yet.

At home, Gloria found a mess in the kitchen and a hungry husband. She refused to cook supper until he washed up.

Gloria considered the bedsit her children shared bleak; she wanted to buy colourful cushions to brighten it up. She would soon need new clothes too and didn't relish trying to justify every item to her husband. Driving home one day she asked Nathan to provide her with a small allowance.

"You want money; you'll have to earn it."

"That's what I was doing before I became your chauffeur," she almost shouted in frustration. Instead, she calmly stated, "I earn it by cooking, cleaning and washing for you and by driving you around. If you don't think I deserve a few pounds to buy myself clothes or gifts for the children, then I'll stop doing all those things and get another job."

"You can't. You're my wife and you've got responsibilities."

"And you're my husband, so do you."

The moment they arrived home, Nathan got out the car, slamming Lucille's door. Gloria drove away. It wasn't long before tears blurred her vision. She pulled over and leant, sobbing, on the steering wheel.

"What am I going to do, Lucille? I can't continue like this."

At thirty-eight, she wasn't too old to change; to be happy. What about Nathan, she wondered, could he change too? She remembered the early days of their marriage. They'd often bought takeaways for supper, because the newlywed couple had better things to do with their evenings than cook. They'd been happy then; what had gone wrong?

She must accept a part of the blame. When she'd become pregnant Nathan had controlled the finances and everything else. Gloria never told him she wasn't happy, with two toddlers she'd lacked the energy for anything other than to do as instructed. Their conversation dwindled to updates on the children and domestic details. They'd both got used to that. Maybe that's how it had been for Lucille's previous owner?

Gloria wiped her eyes; hiding from her husband was no way to save her marriage. She decided to buy a takeaway for supper; she doubted Nathan would have cooked. Perhaps it would remind him of happier times.

At home, Nathan was hysterical. There was foam coming from the washing machine and smoke from the grill. He'd smashed a tankard, shards of broken glass glinted on the floor. There was shoe polish on his sleeve.

"Come and eat your dinner whilst it's hot," Gloria said, taking cutlery and plates into the dining room. "We'll clean this lot up once we've eaten."

"We?"

"Yes, Nathan, we're a married couple, perhaps it's time we acted like it."

She spooned curry onto a plate and handed it to him.

"Thank you, love."

She was so startled she almost dropped the plate. It seemed she was right; there was a chance for them.

"I've taken you for granted, haven't I?" he asked.

"You have, and I've acted like a discontented servant."

"Not any more."

"No, not any more."

"Gloria, the microwave still works, doesn't it?"

"Yes, why?"

Nathan pushed his plate away and stood up. "We could heat this up later." As he made the suggestion he walked towards her and put a hand on her shoulder. "You seem a bit tense."

He gently kneaded her shoulders. After a few moments he

slid his hands inside the loose neck of the cotton sweater and massaged her bare skin. Gloria sighed and arched her back a little.

"Come on," Nathan whispered and took her hand to lead her upstairs.

Later, they ate the reheated curry and grinned at each other.

He said, "We've wasted so much time. I was thinking today about the first car we ever had. Do you remember how we'd kiss every time we had to stop for a red light and how every chance we'd get we'd be driving down a quiet country lane?"

"Yes, I remember." Maybe they wouldn't behave like that again, but it seemed they might regain some of their former happiness.

Gloria also remembered the young man whose mother died in her car. She wanted to thank him for what he'd said, to tell him his mother's car and his words helped her escape from a tragic marriage into a far better one.

The car's logbook showed details of the previous owner. She went to the address and explained she was looking for a relation of Mrs Browne.

"She was my aunt. You do know she's dead?" the lady said.

"Yes, I've come because of her son."

"It was so sad about Lenny, dying so young."

"Dying? What happened?"

"There were rumours that his father bullied my aunt, of course we didn't like to believe them. The way she died suggested there was some truth in them; you knew about that?"

"I knew he was unkind to her, but I don't know what happened to Lenny. Surely his father wasn't responsible for his death?"

"In a way. We now guess that it was his refusal to get medical help for her when she went into labour early that caused things to go wrong at the birth. Lenny survived that, but he was never strong. As he grew up he was often ill, he rarely had the strength to leave the house. He died of pneumonia eventually. Aunty took flowers to his grave every week. I like to think that Aunt Lucille and Lenny are happy and together now."

"I'm sure they are," Gloria said.

"Sorry, but who are you?" Lucille's niece asked.

"A friend of Lucille's. I'm glad to know her son's name; I'll name my new baby after him."

Gloria went home to Nathan. They were starting again and this time they'd do things right.

16. Shadow Dancer

It's October. The time of year when the leaves fall, twisting and twirling. A fouetté of foliage, dance of decay. They leave behind a tracery of limbs to pirouette in the breeze. The street light outside shines through the tree and casts a shadow on the wall.

In summer, as it was when I first saw it, the shadow image is blurry. If the figure performed a relevé or plié, you'd not even notice it unless you knew to look. Even a grand jeté could be missed, unless you wanted to see.

I had wanted to see a dancer when I first came to En Pointe House. Not as a shadow on the wall, but as a reflection in the mirror. Mum couldn't afford lessons for me. A teacher at school spoke to her about scholarships. Mum listened politely and thanked her, but afterwards she shook her head sadly.

"Sorry, love. Not even if they're free," she told me. She smiled. "Free love brought me your pretty mouth to feed. Free ballet lessons would only cost shoes and tutus, but I still can't manage it."

I didn't follow all that, but I did understand she couldn't afford silk pumps for me to wear. Sometimes she couldn't send me to school with more than dry bread for my lunch. When the factory went to a three day week, she couldn't afford the rent either. At the time we were sharing a room in a terrace, just a few doors away from En Pointe House. It was rumoured the owner, whom people referred to as

Mademoiselle, was foreign and very wealthy.

We'd spoken to her a couple of times. She didn't sound foreign. Once Mum saw all her sheets and stuff on the line as it started to rain and we rushed to help bring them in. She'd been grateful, I remembered. So did Mum. In desperation she knocked at Mademoiselle's door and begged her to allow us to use one of her many spare rooms in exchange for Mum cleaning the rest of the house.

"How did it go?" I asked when she returned.

"She clearly didn't know what to say. I don't think she's rich after all, but she does have lots of empty rooms. We're invited to tea tomorrow."

I was smartened up as much as possible and instructed to sit nicely and not speak until I was spoken to. I did try, but when Mademoiselle ushered us in, I saw the shadow on the wall and gasped.

"What did you see, child?" Mademoiselle asked.

"A dancer."

"It's just the shadow of a tree," Mum said.

"Were you a dancer, Mademoiselle? Someone at school said you were."

Mum looked daggers at me for forgetting my manners, but Mademoiselle laughed.

"What did you call me, child?"

"Mademoiselle... I... I thought it was your name."

"No, it means a French woman who isn't married. It's a long story and you're young."

Her name was Juliet, she told us, but she didn't mind me and Mum continuing to use the name we'd come to think of her by.

"The kettle should be boiling now," she said.

Mum went with her to fetch the tea and I tried to sit quietly. I watched the shadow and couldn't resist imitating the graceful shapes created by the shadow figure.

When Mademoiselle saw me attempting the position I now know as first arabesque, she made up her mind. As I ate Battenberg and sipped tea which smelled of perfume, it was arranged that we had a place to live if Mum kept our own rooms and the kitchen and bathroom spotless. Mademoiselle agreed to fund my dance lessons and clothes, if I practised with her for hours and hours and hours.

I almost hated her at first, she made me work so hard. We became friends though. Eventually she told me the story of her French lover. And the one about the lady who'd owned the house before her. She'd once been a principal dancer and had become Mademoiselle's teacher and patron.

"I was poor, poorer even than you when you first came here and not nearly so well brought up. I looked in through the window there, in the hope of seeing anything edible I could grab. The owner saw me attempt to copy the position of the shadow," she said, indicating the tree dancing in the breeze.

Like Mademoiselle, I gained a place in the corps de ballet. I progressed and even danced a few solos. Between each tour I returned to Mum and Mademoiselle. They're both gone now.

It's just me and the shadow in En Pointe House. Or it has been. Last night about this time, the boy next door kicked his ball over the fence. He knocked and asked for permission to retrieve it. Just lately I've been concerned about that family. The father lost his job and the mother is hardly ever there. I watched, unseen by the boy as he fetched his ball and carried it over the lawn onto the patio. Then he dropped it and moved closer to the window. He looked in for a moment, his face pressed against the glass, then moved back. He extended a leg gracefully behind him and raised his arms en haut.

I don't know his story, but the boy and his father are coming to tea on Saturday. I'll know more then and hopefully find a way to help.

Until then, I watch the leaves fall from my tree. They twist and turn in a fouetté of foliage, dance of rebirth. They leave behind a tracery of limbs to pirouette in the breeze. The street light outside shines through the tree and casts a shadow on the wall.

17. Can't Take It With You

"Do you believe in the living?" George asked his wife.

"Of course!" Ethel said. "We were living ourselves once, weren't we?"

"I'm not so sure. People say they've seen and heard livings but I reckon they've just imagined it."

"There's proof," Ethel exclaimed. "Plenty of people remember being alive and some come through with those photo things."

"Hmmmm, I have seen those," George admitted. "But if they're genuine, why have people changed so much? They used to all be in happy groups outside and be black and white. Now they're on their own pouting at bathroom mirrors and they're colourful."

"That's because of technology."

"Oh come on, you can't really believe in technology! Devices so the living can talk to people who're miles away and ignore those who're right next to them? Machines to pump blood or air into people to keep them alive and guns and bombs to send them here?"

"OK, I admit some of it sounds strange, but it's probably because we don't understand. My guess is it's something to do with money."

George shook his head. "Nobody with sense could possibly believe in money. Bits of metal and paper that'll make people stay all day in places they hate, or lie to get, or fall out with family over, yet are just the same as the pieces they already had? The whole idea is just stupid and not a single one of us has ever brought any through, or wanted anything to do with it once they've arrived."

"True," Ethel agreed. "I'm sure I used to want some, but for the death of me I can't think why."

"Excuse me," a messenger interrupted the conversation. "But I have good news for you both."

"Out with it then," George demanded.

"The last of your great-grandsons has just died."

"How old?" Ethel asked.

"103," the messenger said. "He arrived fast asleep, but he's awake now."

"That's good. The sleeping ones always settle in quicker," Ethel remarked.

"Fantastic news," George said. "I must go and meet him and say, 'Welcome to the family'. Coming, Ethel?"

"Of course I am, George. You know, I can remember when he was born."

"I can't," George insisted.

"That'll be because of the beer, love."

"Just a drop to wet his head. Oh…"

"You remember beer then?"

"Absolutely not. Just humouring you."

"Huh! Be the first time in your death you've done that!"

Zac, like all newly-deads, was slightly disorientated so they didn't stay long. His parents and siblings had a greater claim; George and Ethel had all eternity to get to know him.

"I like him," Ethel said as they glided back to their regular spot.

"Me too. Handsome lad, got my nose I think."

"You know what this means, George? He was the last of those living when we were alive."

"If we ever were."

"We can go back and visit the real world."

"If there's such a place."

Ethel continued as though she hadn't heard. "You can find out for yourself if the living are real."

"What if we get stuck?" George lost so much of his sickly pallor he looked almost healthy.

"Don't worry, love," Ethel soothed. "That only happens to a few of those who haven't left their life behind. You've so much given up on yours that you don't believe it happened."

"But you do."

"Yes, but I don't want to go back to it, except just for a look. I'm curious. I wonder if they still have beer?"

"OK, OK next Hallowe'en we'll give it a try, but don't go getting too disappointed if nothing happens."

"Thanks, love." Ethel kissed him.

"George! What possessed you to bring me here?"

"This was your idea! And I'm not possessed... though I'm not so sure about this lot."

George and Ethel huddled together listening to terrible wailing sounds and watching horrible livings dripping blood from their mouths, wearing sheets or dragging chains. Some walked, some lurched as they moved from house to house demanding candy and... could it be? They crept closer. Yes – money! Weirdly though the bats and toads were lifeless, the vegetables, especially pumpkins, seemed to be alive.

George and Ethel tried not to look at their evil grins and the bright lights shining from their eyes.

A group of livings caught sight of George and Ethel. At first the livings waved, laughed and called out words of praise for their shroud costumes. Then when they were right in front of George and Ethel a living stretched out his hand.

"Who's under there?" he asked and lifted Ethel's hood.

He seemed to scream though no sound came out. Two of the others stood still and trembled. The fourth fainted.

"Keep them busy," George muttered. "I have an idea."

Ethel sang, which seemed to do the trick.

George was soon back with a barrel of beer and stack of plastic glasses. "The chap who had this wanted money, but once I explained why I don't have pockets he said to help myself."

Ethel and George set to work persuading their acquaintances to consume several pints of beer apiece.

The livings soon cheered up, as did George who joined in the beer drinking. "Just to be sociable, love," he said. "OK I believe in the living," he admitted a bit later. "But it seems this lot don't want to believe in us. Let's get back to our great-grandson before we scare them any more."

"All right, love. But you'd better leave them a hangover so they can pretend they imagined us."

"More beer… or spirits?"

He laughed so hard Ethel gave up waiting and fetched more beer herself. She also picked up the money she found abandoned after her appearance, intending to keep it as proof the living existed. Like George, Ethel didn't have pockets and must have dropped the money because there was no trace of it once she got home.

18. Ghost In A Brown Suit

Danny wasn't happy. That was nothing new, but this time he had good reason. His parents hadn't let him go to Grandad's funeral. They said there was no point him missing school and getting upset over someone he'd never met.

Dad explained the family had lost touch with Grandad after Danny's gran divorced him.

"Why didn't Mum want to see him, Dad?"

"It's a sad story. There was some kind of accident. Your grandad had been drinking and your mum's twin sister was killed. I don't know much because they never really talk about it."

Danny felt cheated; true he'd never met his grandad, in fact hadn't known he had one until last Wednesday, the day after he died. But wasn't that all the more reason for him to be allowed to say goodbye?

Gran and Mum hadn't wanted to go to the funeral themselves but Dad said they should.

"It won't take long, and if you don't you might regret it. Anyway it's the decent thing to do."

So they'd gone, dropping Danny at school on the way. Danny didn't like school. He was doing OK at lessons but, as he'd just started at secondary school and his former classmates had gone to a different one, he hadn't got any friends. The other boys let him tag along, but he didn't have much in common with his sports mad peers. If he'd known his grandad then he'd have taught him to save goals, hold up a scrum or bowl a googly. Now it was too late.

As Danny walked home he saw that man was there again, watching the house. He was wearing the same suit; light brown with an orange tie. Danny saw him first last Tuesday when he came home from school.

"Hello, lad," he'd said.

"I don't talk to strangers," Danny replied as he rushed indoors. The next day the man stood across the road, just looking at his house. Danny thought he looked like the scruffy man who sometimes slept in the park and who'd wanted to talk to the boys. They always kept well away because men who tried to talk to boys in the park were probably bad. The man watching the house looked nearly the same but was clean and tidy. Perhaps he was a relative, looking for the scruffy man. Danny couldn't help anyway, he'd not been seen for several days now.

When the family got back from the funeral, Danny asked about his grandad.

"I don't want to talk about him, love, it makes me sad," Mum said.

"Can I show him the album?" Dad asked.

Dad showed Danny pictures of Mum when she was a little girl. In some there were two little girls who looked just the same. In those pictures there was a man and woman too. In later ones there was only one girl and no man.

Danny looked at the pictures. Then he went over to the window and looked out. "Dad, who's that man, watching the house?" he asked.

"Where?" Dad frowned as he came over to look where Danny pointed. "There's no one there, son, just a shadow."

Danny looked again. Dad was right.

On Saturday Danny went to the park. A boy down the road had heard about his grandad dying and invited him to play football with his friends. The man, the tidy one, was there. Something about him being there made Danny join in the game instead of just watching. He wasn't very good, but one time he passed the ball to a boy who scored.

The scorer clapped him on the back and said, "Nice one, mate."

Danny felt proud and he was sure the man in the brown suit had seen his contribution to the game. Afterwards Danny walked over to him. He knew he shouldn't really, but there were lots of people about and he wasn't going to accept sweets or anything stupid like that. Anyway, family aren't strangers, even if you've never met them.

"Hello."

"I thought you didn't speak to strangers."

"I don't, but I talk to my grandad."

"So you know all about me."

"No, I've only just heard of you. Are you a ghost now?"

"Yes, I suppose so."

"Did you kill Mum's sister and now you have to walk the earth in torment?"

"I didn't kill her, but I suppose I must be in torment. I can't leave here until things are put right. Will you help me?"

"Perhaps... if you tell me what happened."

"Your gran and my daughters were upstairs. The girls were getting dressed up in your gran's clothes. They wore one of her dresses each, her shoes and jewellery. Your gran put some make-up on them and was doing their hair."

"Why?"

"It was just something they liked to do. To tell the truth I was sulking, they often did girlie things together and I felt left out. I poured myself a drink, then another."

"And then you killed her."

"No! No, of course not. Millie, your aunt, tried on your gran's wedding veil. Your mum wanted to try it and snatched at it. Millie ran away, your mum chased her. They were still wearing the heeled shoes and fell down the stairs. Millie hit her head. I called an ambulance; I couldn't drive her to the hospital because I'd been drinking. She was dead when she arrived at hospital. Your gran thought if I'd have driven her there it would have been quicker and she might have lived. She never got over the anger or grief and divorced me."

"Did Mum blame you too?"

"Yes. I tried to visit, but neither of them spoke to me again. I started drinking more and more. I blamed myself too you see. Before long I wasn't fit to be a dad anyway."

"So how are you going to put things right?"

"I don't know. All I can think of is to stay close to you all. Perhaps someday I'll be able to help and then I'll be released. I just hope I can do it in time."

"In time for what?"

"A spirit can only walk the earth for a year and a day. Then it's either up or down."

Danny was thoughtful as he went home. His grandad would be around now, with plenty of time to spend with him. He liked the idea of a grandad to take him for walks, teach him to skim stones or play him at conkers. Grandad promised to do all that and more. It would be fun and they'd have lots of time, school holidays started in just a week. But Danny was too old just to expect his grandad to do things for him. He was old enough to help.

"Grandad, I have an idea. You're stuck here because you didn't save your daughter, aren't you?"

"I suppose so."

"Well if you saved another child that might make up for it."

"Maybe, but how am I supposed to achieve that?"

"We could make some money for Save the Children."

"I'm not sure that would do it."

"We'll try until we think of something better."

On the first day of the school holiday Danny didn't play football with his new friends; he tidied his room. He sorted out all the clothes and games he no longer used and put them into a bag. His mum was pleased and surprised.

"What are you going to do with them?"

"Give them to Save the Children."

"There's not one of them in the town here, I'll take them into Oxfam for you."

"No, it must be Save the Children."

"Why?"

"Because we have to save a child to make up." He stopped talking, he'd seen past his mother, through the window and across the road. Grandad was shaking his head. "I just want to help save a child."

"Oxfam gives food to children. That saves them from starving."

"OK then. Thanks, Mum."

Mum took the stuff to the shop, but a week later Grandad was still a ghost. Danny wasn't too sad about that because Grandad showed him lots of different ways to bowl a cricket ball. They went walking together and Grandad told him which birds were singing.

One day they picked wild flowers, which Danny took home for Mum. She looked sad and happy at the same time when Danny showed her which were milkmaids, cow parsley, dandelions and buttercups.

"My dad used to take me and Millie to pick flowers for your gran."

"I'll get her some too, Mum," Danny promised. He thought Grandad would like to help him do that.

The next day as they walked towards the meadow, Danny noticed a girl from his school sitting, with her legs dangling over the edge of a bridge, looking down into the water.

"What's loony Laura doing up there?"

Grandad looked. "Why do you call her that? It's not a nice thing to say."

"Sorry, Grandad. It's what everyone calls her because she's a goth and looks more like a ghost than you do. She hangs around churchyards because she says she prefers the dead to the living."

"It looks to me as if she intends to join them."

"I'm not sure she'll really jump." Danny thought for a minute. "She's got scars on her arms, people say she cuts herself."

"Poor child."

"Perhaps I should introduce you. She'd probably love to meet a real dead person."

"I don't think she'll see me."

"Let's try, it might cheer her up."

Grandad shrugged and followed Danny onto the bridge.

"Hi, Laura."

"Leave me alone."

"I just want to talk," Danny said.

"Well, I don't. Oh don't worry, Danny, I'm not going to jump. You won't have me on your conscience."

Danny looked at Grandad, but he just waved his hand as though he thought Danny should keep talking.

"What you doing then?"

"Just watching the water."

"Why are you always so unhappy?"

"I'm not unhappy, just mad. I can see dead people. No one believes it. Sometimes even I don't believe it half the time. Then I see them and they ask me for help. I can't help them or myself so it's driving me mad."

Danny nodded. He was worried he hadn't yet found a way to help Grandad. It must be awful to have lots of people needing your help and not be able to do anything.

"Do you see them all the time?"

"Most of the time. I try to ignore them. If you tell someone there's a man in a brown suit and orange tie stood watching them they tend not to like it."

"You can't help what you see, Laura. Just because other people don't see the same thing doesn't make you mad," Danny said.

"So why don't they see them?"

"Perhaps they're not looking."

"And why am I looking?"

"Because you're not happy, because you don't have any living friends."

"No one speaks to me."

"Yeah they do, you just don't listen. Come on, get up. It's

too cold to sit out here."

"It is a bit."

"Get home and I'll see you at school tomorrow and I'll make sure I talk to you."

"Really?"

"Yes. I promise."

Laura stood and walked away, passing right through Grandad as though she could no longer see him. Danny watched her go. It was hard to tell from behind, but he thought she looked happier.

"Why didn't you say you could see me too?" Grandad asked.

"She needs normal friends. Seeing dead people isn't normal, is it?"

Grandad smiled. "So, you'll be her friend?"

"If she'll let me."

Grandad faded away. He smiled and waved as he went.

19. Does Your Mother Know?

I suppose really Mum didn't get more restrictive once I hit my teens, I just resented it more. I was the age where I liked to wander round town with my friends looking into shops and out for boys. If a group of lads approached and suggested we go bowling with them, or off for a walk or anything I couldn't go, not unless every one of them had been through security clearance. If I went to a party or to a disco and a boy offered to walk me home, I had to decline. If he wanted to take me out some other time, he'd have to present himself first for Mum's inspection and offer a flight plan of the evenings activities.

As you can imagine, I didn't go on many dates.

My friends teased me. Before we went anywhere or did anything they'd ask, "Does your mother know?" I blamed ABBA for that, but I guess they'd have teased anyway. They were happy enough to accept a lift home from her though, when she came to pick me up.

I've made Mum sound a bit of a military dictator and that's how it felt at times, but she wasn't all bad. I thought she was just over protective and old fashioned until we were warned at school about a series of attacks on girls. Warned so tactfully I wasn't sure if the attacker would flash at us, steal from us or worse.

Half kidding myself it was to protect her from worry, I considered keeping it from Mum, despite the note we'd each been given to take home. Mostly though it was because I feared being put into lock-down and never let out the house without her. Someone was bound to tell her though, or it would be on the news or in the paper. Playing it down as much as possible, I told her.

She took hold of my hand. "That's why I'm so careful of you always. Pound to a penny those girls were out on their own somewhere they either weren't supposed to be, or had gone off without telling anyone."

"You can't blame them."

"Of course the blame lies with whoever did this, but it's only sensible not to make it easy for him."

It turned out the reports of the attacks hadn't been clear because the attacker's motives weren't. One girl was robbed, but another left with a purse full of money and a good watch on her wrist. Several of the attacks were sexually violent. After reading the graphic accounts in the paper I was as careful of my safety as Mum was. My friends were more cautious too. That lasted until we reached the sixth form.

Then I met Adam Byront. He was a few years older, drop dead gorgeous and way cool. Predictably Mum's reaction to him was 'no'. I begged and pleaded. She was having none of it. Adam didn't give in so easily. Wherever I went he seemed to turn up. He'd dance with me, buy me drinks, take me outside and kiss me. He tried to get me to meet him on his own, or go off with him away from my friends or walk home with him. I couldn't of course. He didn't like that.

Mum began picking me up more often. She seemed to have a sixth sense where Adam was involved. There was never the slightest chance of snogging with him at the bus stop, as the minute the party or disco finished and I stepped outside, there she'd be waiting. There was no way I'd have got away with arriving from round the corner rather than the front door. I imagined her lying in wait from the moment I went in, just in case I tried to slip out for a moment or two off agenda.

Adam met me after school a couple of times. My friends giggled around us for a while, then went on ahead. They weren't even out of sight when Mum 'just happened' to pass by and told me to get in the car.

I was angry with Mum. Looking back I should have wondered why he was so keen to get me on my own. I wasn't ready for more than kissing and I was uncomfortable leaving the safety of whichever venue Mum knew me to be in. Adam said it was just because I'd led such a sheltered life. I blamed Mum for that. Stealing moments alone with Adam became almost a game.

There were more attacks. The police thought they were connected with the earlier ones. It was scary to think this man had been hanging around our little town for a couple of years preying on women and nobody knew who he was. He could be anyone. I knew that in theory, but my schoolgirl heart didn't think it could be anyone I'd ever meet or knew already.

My friends and I all became much more safety conscious again. None of us went off on our own. If we'd have considered it, whoever we were with would have talked us out of it, not least because they themselves didn't want to be left without a friend to ensure they got home safely.

Adam lost interest in me eventually. I was heartbroken for days and directed my misery at Mum for much longer. Then I met Mike. He passed Mum's test, whatever it was. We married and I had my own daughter. I told myself I wouldn't hold her back as my mum had held me back; right up until the time I realised Mum never had. She'd kept me safe and taught me to be careful.

Some of the children at Chloe's school seemed dubious to me. I would have forgiven Mum then if she'd stopped me being friends with kids like them, but other than Adam she'd never rejected my choices. What colour their skin was, whether their parents had jobs and where they lived didn't worry her as long as she was allowed to meet them and assess them. I went on Guide camp, and sleepovers and even a week's exchange in France. Mum checked up on the arrangements, but she let me go.

Chloe's skirts seemed too short and her heels too high. I wanted to tell her not to go out looking like that. I remembered Mum never passed judgement on shorts so short I had to be careful which knickers I wore or they'd show, and shirts which had more buttons done up on the sleeves than down the front. When I wore so much eye make-up winking was a mini workout she hardly even raised an eyebrow. She let me out looking like that, just not on my own.

I said nothing negative about Chloe's outfits, ensuring only that she was always with friends when she went out, had transport home arranged and stayed safe. I saw Mum had only wanted to keep me safe and told her so.

"I'll always keep you safe, my love," she said.

That comforted me at the time, even though I saw how frail she was. For a time after her death it continued to comfort me. She'd approved of Mike and rather encouraged our marriage. She'd helped financially toward the purchase of our home. She'd set a good example in raising a daughter.

Mike was a good husband. Reliable, dependable. I had a lovely daughter going off to university. Maybe it was some kind of middle-age crisis or the shock of losing Mum, but I suddenly craved the excitement and danger I'd never experienced.

Mike was away on a business trip and Chloe at uni. I borrowed her heels and skirt and went clubbing. Yeah, I know I probably doubled the average age just by walking in there, but I wanted to dance. We've got plush carpet everywhere at home. Lovely for walking barefoot on, rubbish for throwing a few shapes to a banging tune. I didn't tell anyone where I was going and, as I didn't know how long I'd want to stay, I didn't order a taxi home. And what prompted this stupidity? Another attack. Well not so much that as the warning on the local news, that came after the report, about staying safe. They repeated all the stuff Mum had insisted on. Then a reporter did one of those on the street things asking local women what they thought. Did they worry about going out alone, or their daughter's doing so? It seemed to me we were all being encouraged to live in fear. Not me I decided, I wasn't going to stay afraid.

The nightclub occupied the spot which held the weekly disco when I'd been a teenager. Maybe that gave me a false sense of security. Walking in felt like walking back in time and when I noticed Adam Byront I thought it was my imagination playing tricks. He was as handsome as ever, he hardly seemed to have changed at all. He made a beeline for me and I was flattered thinking he remembered me. We danced and he bought me drinks. I was out of practice with drinking and it rather went to my head. I didn't feel well and told Adam I needed air. I think I was sick, but I don't really remember.

Then I was at Adam's flat, not sure how I'd got there. Just suddenly aware I was alone with him in what was clearly a bachelor pad and he was telling me I needed another drink. I was sure I didn't but couldn't seem to speak or do anything much. He left the room and I sat staring ahead, my unfocussed attention on a photograph. It seemed vital to know who or what it was of. I struggled to my feet, staggered over and reached up for it. In one of those curved glass frames was a picture of Mum. I gripped it tightly and listened as she told me to leave. The fright made me feel sick again. I threw up. I pulled open a window, leant out and fell onto the grass; thank goodness he lived on the ground floor.

There was another blank then until the next morning when I came to, still in Chloe's skirt, on my bed. Her shoes were ruined and my head felt worse than they looked. I was so ashamed of what I'd done. Risked my marriage by potentially embarking on an affair with Adam. Well that wouldn't happen now as embarrassment at being sick in his home then running away would ensure I avoided him in future, even if I'd really been tempted. I'd risked my safety too. If the attacker had found me between leaving Adam's place and getting home there would have been nothing I could have done to fend him off.

I tried to forget all about the incident. I threw out Chloe's shoes telling her I'd tried them on just to see if I could walk in them and couldn't and broke a heel. She found it very funny, partly because I promised I'd buy her another pair.

Chloe, back from her first term at university, decided she and her lovely new shoes should go clubbing. The attacker still hadn't been caught, but even without that I'm sure I'd have insisted we pick her up.

As Mike and I sat waiting, I saw Adam come out with a woman. She was so drunk he had to hold her upright. Fresh shame flooded over me as I watched them. Not so long ago that had been me. Clearly he made a habit of this kind of thing. Had he even realised who I was? He hadn't asked my name that I could recall, but it could have been because he didn't care. I'd probably meant no more to him than this other woman. At a quick glance we probably even looked similar. Her hair was a little shorter and blonder than mine and the skirt a little longer. Maybe it was her own and not her teenage daughter's?

"All right?" Mike asked.

Realising I'd been staring at Adam and his woman I assured him I was. Chloe came out then and we took her home.

Next day on the news there was a report of another attack. A woman had left the nightclub just before Chloe. Her body, when they found it, revealed she'd been drugged first, then attacked, then dumped and left to die. It had been an unusually warm night and a dog walker discovered her very early the following morning or she'd have been dead.

I remembered how sick I'd been after just a couple of drinks in the nightclub. I hardly needed to see the CCTV footage of her leaving the nightclub to know it was the woman I'd seen. Adam was the attacker. I know you'd guessed already, but perhaps you can understand why I'd been so unwilling to make the connection.

The police were very kind. That they believed me was a relief as I'd worried I'd be confessing my stupidity for nothing. They said they'd try to keep my name out of any press reports, but couldn't guarantee it. Deciding that if he were to hear about it at all, it'd be better coming from me, I gave Mike a toned down version of events. He took it pretty well, all things considered.

I told the police all the facts I could remember. It didn't seem much, but thankfully there weren't many flats in town in which it was possible to fall out the ground floor living-room window onto grass. Only one of those was occupied by one of their suspects.

Rain had washed away all traces of my footprints, but when I was taken to the scene I looked through the window and knew it was the right place.

"That's enough for a search warrant, I think, but it will help the case if we can prove you were in there."

I remembered the picture of Mum. It couldn't really have been of her of course and it was the spiked drink that made me think it had spoken. I had really touched it though. They found my fingerprints on the glass frame and traces of my vomit, drugs included, in his carpet.

Did Mum, wherever she is, know she saved me? I might never know, but I know she kept me safe.

20. World's Best Sister

"Happy birthday, Gran," Natalie whispered as she stepped out into the garden. Might as well say it there as anywhere else. There was no proper place to remember her, thanks to Felicity being so unreasonable!

A splash of bright orange, Gran's favourite colour, caught her attention. There was a broken mug in the flower bed. How could that have got there? Natalie spotted 'World's Best Sister' on the side. She hadn't thought it was hers, but that confirmed it. Sadly she'd never had reason to give, or receive, such a thing.

Natalie and Felicity had never got on. They'd hardly ever tried. The only times they came close had been on Gran's birthday. Maybe, in her memory, she should try again? Natalie went back in, looked up the number and called. She couldn't help feeling relieved at getting the answerphone.

"Hi, Natalie here. Just thought I'd call and well, say hello. Um, hope you're all OK. We are. Speak later maybe."

That was a bit rubbish, but probably nicer than anything else she'd said to her sister.

"Who was that, love?" Mark asked.

"Felicity."

"Something wrong?"

"No, I called her… just to say hi."

The surprise on her husband's face that she'd call her sister for anything so trivial, so pleasant, said a lot. How had they got like that?

Actually Natalie disliked her younger sister even before she was born. At six years old she'd worked out the love and attention which had been exclusively hers would have to be shared. Perhaps if Mum hadn't died in childbirth she'd have eventually realised the love wouldn't be halved but doubled. Natalie had never shared anything with Felicity, not even her grief.

Gran helped their dad, her son-in-law, raise them. Mostly that involved refereeing arguments between the girls. What a waste of her time when she'd simply wanted to love and care for them both. The girls had fought so badly that Natalie often stayed with Gran whilst Felicity remained with Dad. They'd brought about the division and sharing of love and attention which Natalie had feared and surely neither of them had wanted.

Gran and Dad had done their best, ensuring the girls spent some time together and at least pretended to be civil, but it wasn't fun for any of them. Worst perhaps for Gran because although she'd helped separate them for the best of reasons, she blamed herself for the split. The sisters hadn't blamed her but each other, as always.

They'd argued more fiercely than ever over where to scatter Gran's ashes.

Dad had picked up the urn. "I'm keeping these until you both agree."

"That's not fair! She's not your mum," Felicity had said.

"There's a lot that's not fair in this life and you two constantly arguing is one of them."

He was right; Felicity's suggested locations had been just as appropriate as her own, but she'd refused to even consider them. She'd upset Dad, not put Gran to rest, and made herself miserable just to spite her sister. How often had she hurt herself and others for the same reason?

She remembered the mug and went out to pick up the pieces before anyone cut themselves on the sharp edges. Strange, it wasn't actually broken after all, just cracked and caked in mud.

"You ready, love?" Mark called.

"Coming." She left the mug on the patio, where it was out of the way.

When they returned from shopping, there was a message from Felicity. 'Thanks for calling. Yes we're all fine. Glad to hear you are too. We really should… well, um, bye for now.'

They really should what? Decide what to do with Gran's ashes? Yes, they should. Or maybe she meant they should talk? Yes, they should do that too. They never had, not properly. They'd gone to each other's weddings and met at Dad's and Gran's homes over the years but not frequently. So much they'd missed out on, all of them.

Mark came in, carrying the orange mug. "Did you know this was in the garden?"

"Yes, I found it smashed in the flower bed. No, not smashed, just cracked."

"Not even that, I don't think."

She saw he was right. It was quite grubby, but would be fine if given a scrub. It was a lovely shape and a cheerful colour, perhaps it would be worth the effort.

"I'll put it in to soak," Mark asked.

"Yes, OK… I think I'll ring Felicity back." She did start to dial, but chickened out halfway through and sent a text instead. 'I know it's short notice, but today is a good day to scatter Gran's ashes don't you think? You suggested the beach at Hayling Island. We can do it there if you like.'

Felicity's reply came swiftly. 'I'm free to do it today and it does seem right. I know you wanted to do it at Porchester Castle. That's fine with me.'

They agreed to meet each other halfway, at Staunton Park. Then Natalie rang Dad to check it was OK to collect Gran's ashes.

"Yes, if you come together."

When they did just that, he hugged them both. Sharing the love.

They drove to the park separately, but there was no racing ahead or fighting over who carried the urn. They left their cars side by side and walked together across the grass. They didn't say much as they selected a location, murmured goodbye to Gran and sprinkled her ashes over the daisies and buttercups. The silence felt respectful, rather than hostile.

"Do you have to get back straight away?" Natalie asked, though unsure exactly why.

"No... but if you're not in a hurry either, we could go back to mine for a cup of tea. I baked a fudge cake using Gran's recipe and I know you like it."

"That would be great. Thank you."

As Felicity filled the teapot, Natalie saw an orange mug, left to soak in her sister's kitchen sink. It looked very familiar and she reached her hand into the water and picked it up. Sure enough, 'World's Best Sister' was written on the side.

"Oh! I'm sorry about that. I didn't mean for you to see it, honestly. I found it this morning..."

"Buried in mud in the garden?"

Felicity shook her head. "I know it sounds mad, but it was hanging in a tree. I just stepped into the garden to say happy birthday to Gran and there it was. At first I thought it was broken, but…"

"It seems even more odd once you know I found an identical one at probably the same moment."

"But… Gran?"

"I don't know, but since we've both got one of these, how about we call a truce and try to go some way to deserving them?"

"Deal. Cut the cake will you, while I pour?"

Not so long ago her reaction would have been to refuse, or argue. Instead Natalie pulled the cake tin towards her and prised off the lid. Felicity had made a good job of the cake, but as nice as it looked, it would bring them both much more pleasure once divided and shared.

The sisters raised their teacups and in unison said, "Happy Birthday, Gran."

21. Blood-Red Christmas Baubles

"Wait a second," I whisper.

Mum stops and rushes round to crouch in front of my chair.

I look at her tear-stained face. "Just pull me back a bit will you?"

I bend down and pick up a shard of Christmas bauble. Even that small effort leaves me breathless. The crimson glass sparkles in my hand. Does it mean life for me or death for all of us? For the first time I realise it's the colour of blood. Fresh, healthy blood. The broken fragment is in the shape of a heart. Running over the surface is a filigree of gold. When the baubles were whole they were patterned with intricate snowflakes. Now the delicate strands remind me of blood vessels carrying oxygen rich blood. Life giving blood.

It's my imagination of course. When you're waiting for a transplant it's hard to think of anything else.

It's not nice waiting for someone to die. Hoping it will happen. That was me. That was my family. We wanted a stranger to die so I could live.

Mum decided to make a big deal of Christmas. All the family, happy together. I wished she wouldn't. Really, really wished she wouldn't. I just knew something would go wrong. Maybe it was because I knew it might be the last. Mine or maybe Grandma's.

"What would you like to eat, love? Traditional, or

something else?" Mum asked.

I wasn't bothered. Doing nothing but sit in a wheelchair didn't give me much of an appetite. Mum looked hurt at my lack of enthusiasm so I pretended an interest in turkey and sprouts. Mum's the sort who buys cranberry sauce in October just in case the shops run out.

Tell the truth, once it was settled I started looking forward to the sort of Christmas I'd enjoyed when I was a kid. I asked for a real tree to set off Grandma's heirloom Christmas baubles; pretty, delicate and a proper Christmassy red.

At first everything seemed fine. Grandma was happy to be escaping the home for a few days to stay with us. My kid brother Keith agreed to spend time with us instead of being constantly round at his girlfriend's, Mum didn't have a meltdown over menu plans and Dad got out of being on call for the garage.

Mum decided not to finish decorating the tree until Grandma was there. She had some idea of us all putting on a bauble at the same time.

"How's that going to work?" I'd asked. "There will only be five of us."

It wasn't until the words were out that I remembered. There were only five baubles left. Uncle Jimmy had smashed one, just the day before the motorcycle accident which killed him. I shivered at the memory. Uncle Jimmy had been larking about, as he so often did. He'd pretended he was going to juggle the baubles as he removed them from the tree on twelfth night. Grandma had yelled at him not to be so stupid. One fell from his fingers and smashed. The following day his motorcycle skidded on a patch of ice. He died on the way to the hospital.

Not long after that Grandma had gone into a home. Most

of her stuff was sold, or given away. A few nice things, including the baubles, she gave to Mum.

"Keep them safe, promise me."

Even at the time I'd thought it odd she'd seemed so much more concerned with their safety than with the fate of her other things.

"She's a bit superstitious," Mum said.

That satisfied me then, but as we prepared for Christmas I wondered. Grandma hadn't been nearly so worried about the huge mirror she and Grandad had as a wedding present. My suspicions grew stronger when Grandma was told about the plan to put up the red baubles.

"I think it would be safer to keep them where they are." She looked pale, as pale as me.

"They're here," Mum said and showed Grandma the box.

"They're so pretty, Grandma," I said as persuasively as I could. "It seems a shame not to use them."

"Well, as they're out already," Grandma conceded. She took the box herself and gently removed a bauble which she gave to Mum. Once it was on the tree, she took another which she offered to my brother. I'm not quite sure how but it fell.

"Sorry, Grandma," Keith said.

"No! You didn't drop it, I did. I did! Don't you dare say different."

I knew then I'd been right; there was something strange about the baubles.

"Look, it's OK," Dad said.

He picked up the intact decoration and gave it back to Keith. Once Keith had put it in place Dad held out his hand for a bauble. Grandma gave it to him and took one for herself. Then it was my turn.

Dad wheeled me close to the tree. Grandma gave me a bauble, then kept her hands cupped under mine as I attached it to the tree. Once the five baubles were securely in place Grandma seemed to relax.

Later that evening, Mum, Dad and Keith went out to watch fireworks. It was too cold for me to fancy it and Grandma said she too would rather stay in. The minute we were alone I asked her why she was so worried about the baubles.

"They're very old and very fragile."

"I know, but they're just glass. When Keith smashed your crystal vase that time you weren't angry with him, just worried he might cut himself on the splintered pieces."

"Yes, well…"

A memory came to me, Grandma angry at our neighbour because he'd answered the phone in the middle of a DIY project, leaving a drill connected up and in reach of me and Keith.

"The only times you get angry are when it's people, not things, that might be harmed."

Grandma said nothing.

"There's something about those baubles, isn't there?"

She nodded, or perhaps simply dropped her head in defeat.

"Because of Uncle Jimmy?"

She drew in a long, slow breath. "No, what happened to him was because of the baubles. There used to be twelve, when your great-great-grandparents had them."

"What happened to them?"

"Second year they had them one got smashed as they were put away. The following day the baby died."

"How sad."

"She'd been very ill, it wasn't really a surprise... but yes, sad."

"Which left eleven baubles?"

"Yes, for a few years. Then the family moved home. Two baubles got smashed and right after your great-grandad and his oldest son were killed when a mine shaft collapsed."

"Leaving nine."

"My baby brother died in early January one year. Measles."

"You can't die from measles."

"You can if you're not vaccinated. That didn't come in until just after then."

"The baubles?" I whispered.

"When they came to put them away they found one was broken."

"Eight."

"My mum died at Christmas. They had a cat and it seems that had played with the decorations and smashed one. It also damaged the lights and Mum was electrocuted."

Why oh why had I asked for the baubles to be put up?

"Your dad died very soon after didn't he?" I asked.

"Yes. Of a broken heart I'm sure."

"But not a broken bauble?"

"Oh yes, that too. He broke it himself. After that I decided not to tell anyone about the... curse, I suppose you'd call it."

I tried to ignore my growing fear. "But, Grandma, it can't really be true. Lots more than seven people have died in our family in all that time. Grandad, your brothers, uncles and aunts…"

"Yes, of course."

"You can't believe it," I said though it was myself I was trying to convince. "If you did you'd have had them locked away in a vault somewhere."

"It's not that simple. People have died, yes. The years a person died in their beds of old age were years the baubles were put on the tree and then packed away again safely. Every time they weren't brought out, someone from the family was lost too early, the following year."

"You didn't want them put out this year. Was that for me? You thought one might break and I'd die before twelfth night?'

"Yes, love."

I barely caught her answer.

"But then someone would die next year."

"I'm old, love."

"That's why you said you'd dropped one when it was Keith? But it's OK, it didn't break. We'll all be OK. I'll get my operation."

"Maybe. I hope so, love."

The others came in from the fireworks then. They'd drunk mulled wine and were in festive mood so we sang carols. Well, the four others did. I didn't have the breath for it.

Christmas was good really. We even managed to get Mum out of the kitchen long enough to open her presents and eat her lunch. It was a peaceful few days. No snowball fights, long walks along the beach or anything else I'd have had to miss. For New Year's Eve Keith went to his girlfriend's, Mum and Dad went to a work do and Grandma said she'd sit up to see the New Year in. I offered to stay with her.

"No, love. Look you're nearly asleep now. You let me help you into bed."

My thoughts were optimistic as I drifted to sleep. A New Year ahead and hopefully it would bring me a new heart, a new life. I didn't hear anything until Mum came into my room the next morning.

"Happy New Year," I started to say. Then I saw her expression.

"It's your grandma. She's dead." Mum sat on my bed and held my hand.

"But she can't be! The baubles didn't break." Grandma was old though, maybe it had just been her time and nothing to do with the curse.

"What do you mean?"

"Just something Grandma said on Christmas Eve."

"She's been funny about them ever since Jimmy... Maybe that's why?"

"What, Mum? How did she die?"

"I... I suppose you'll have to know. She took sleeping tablets. All of them. She took the old red baubles from the tree, smashed every one and then swallowed the tablets. It doesn't make any sense."

It did to me, but it didn't seem the time to explain. Then there wasn't time. Keith came home. Doctor, police, undertakers crowded into the house. Mum dressed me and helped me downstairs. Dad offered to do it, but I don't think Mum wanted to be left with time to think. That was left to me. Five smashed baubles, one member of the family dead. Was that the end of the curse?

Once the officials and Grandma's body were gone the

house fell quiet. When the phone rang we all jumped, but no one seemed to want to answer it.

"It'll be OK," I said. We were all safe at home. It couldn't be bad news about one of us.

It wasn't. The hospital had a heart, could I go in straight away? Dad rushed out to scrape the ice off the car. Keith ran up for the bag I had packed ready. Mum helped me into my chair and pushed me toward the door.

What do the smashed baubles mean? I looked around me hoping for some kind of sign or reassurance.

"Wait a second," I whisper.

Mum stops and I bend down for the heart shaped shard of red glass. I keep hold of it as I'm helped into the car and we, all four of us, drive to the hospital. Five smashed baubles, just one death. Icy roads, the need to arrive as soon as possible. The end of the curse, or are we setting off on our final journey?

22. The Wedding Guest

Erin and Jude thanked the vicar and left the church hand in hand. Walking through the graveyard on a winter's evening might have seemed a little creepy under different circumstances but Erin's mind was full of happy thoughts. Their wedding date was set, hymns and vows chosen, bell-ringers booked and the number for the lady who did the flowers in her pocket.

"It's all going to be so perfect," she said.

Jude pulled her to him for a kiss. "I'm glad you talked me into doing the whole church thing now," he said.

"Really?"

"Really. Mostly because I see how much it means to you, but it feels right."

Erin heard the crunch of footsteps on the gravel path. What looked like a witch walked towards them. She wore a long black coat, big hat and assortment of scarves. Her face was so pale it seemed to glow like the moon. As she drew closer, it was clear she was just an ordinary old woman, wrapped up well against the cold.

She nodded at them as she passed.

Jude gave her a cheery greeting, but Erin shivered. The woman looked just like old Muriel. Seeing her the day they'd arranged their wedding service didn't feel like a good omen.

"You OK?" Jude asked.

Erin nodded uncertainly. Should she tell her fiancé about

the old woman's history?

"Do you know her?" His question answered her own.

"Sort of. Her name's Muriel and she haunts weddings."

"Haunts? You mean she's a ghost?"

"I don't know. I mean no, of course not. There's no such thing and anyway, ghosts don't go to church, do they?"

"So, what's up?"

"She goes to all the local weddings and gives me the creeps. I don't like the idea of her being at ours."

Maybe she wouldn't go? Although it seemed the old woman went to every wedding in the church that probably wasn't the case. True she'd been to every wedding Erin had attended there, but that gave a total of four, no five, times. Several relations had got married there when Erin was little and she'd been a bridesmaid to three of them. Muriel had definitely been there for those.

"Is she a relation or something? Someone we'll have to invite?" Jude asked.

"No and not inviting her won't make any difference. She just comes and watches the service. I don't think you're allowed to ban people doing that and anyway it wouldn't seem right. She didn't cause any trouble or anything like that, just stood quietly at the back and watched."

"Doesn't sound too sinister."

"Actually, sometimes she was quite helpful. She knew where the spare hymn books were if more were needed, reassured nervous bridesmaids they looked lovely, let the guests know when she saw the bridal car arrive and if litter had blown about she picked it up so it didn't spoil photos. She did all that without a word, just a smile or nod."

"She never speaks? That does sound a bit ghostly. You

think she's bad luck? Have all the weddings she's been at ended in divorce?"

"No, actually they're all together."

"Maybe she's good luck then?"

"Yes, perhaps." She didn't believe it though.

Erin told herself she was being silly. The thought of poor Muriel's sadness was the real problem; she knew why Muriel was so keen to watch weddings.

The last time Erin had attended a wedding in the church had been a year ago. She'd moved out of her parents' home a few years previously, and although she visited them often she felt a bit of a stranger in the village where she'd grown up. It had been a pleasant surprise to see Muriel at the back of the church. A reminder some things didn't change.

After the service Erin had sought out the old woman and chatted to her while the pictures were being taken.

"I remember you being a flower girl here, don't I and a bridesmaid?" Muriel asked.

"That's right. I remember you too. It seemed you went to every wedding here."

"I do, yes. I love to watch them. Never had my day in church, do you see? I was going to, had begun making my dress, then the war started."

"Oh, I'm so sorry."

"Ah well, it was a long time ago."

Erin was called to be in a photo at that point and hadn't spoken to Muriel again. She saw her though, smiling broadly as she watched the pictures being taken and then the bride and groom get into the car to drive to the reception.

Erin again wondered what happened. Was her fiancé called up and killed in action before he could get back?

Maybe he'd already been in the army and they'd planned to get wed when he was on leave, but the war meant it was cancelled. Maybe a bomb... Or perhaps Jude was right and she was a ghost and the bridegroom-to-be was killed in the Charge of the Light Brigade or something. Erin didn't want to think about it. She shivered again.

"Nearly at your parents now," Jude reassured her. "Your mum will have the kettle on and be waiting to hear all the details."

He was right and Erin almost forgot about Old Muriel until they attended a service to hear their banns read. Muriel was there and was amongst those who turned to smile at Erin and Jude. She looked genuinely pleased for them.

After church, many members of the congregation congratulated them. "We hope you'll be as happy as we are," was a common sentiment. Muriel didn't join in the crush around them, but she smiled again.

"Was that your ghost lady?" Jude asked.

"Who?" Erin's mum asked.

Jude pointed to where they'd seen Muriel standing, but she'd vanished.

Erin kept thinking about the old lady as they walked back to enjoy a traditional Sunday roast with her parents. There was no doubt Muriel liked weddings. She wasn't just torturing herself at the ones where Erin had seen her. Muriel's eyes sparkled as the church bells rang, she wiped away a happy tear when the newly married pair kissed. It was such a shame someone like that hadn't had her own wedding in the church.

Later, she suggested to Jude, "Let's invite Muriel to our wedding."

"If it'll make you happy, then of course we'll invite a ghost to our wedding."

"She's not a ghost, you know that."

"I don't know. She never speaks and no one else seems to see her and…"

"She does speak," Erin informed him. She regretted it when he wanted to know what she'd said.

"That'd explain her haunting the church whenever there's anything to do with weddings. Maybe only people who marry there can see her?"

It would be easy enough to ask her parents if they knew who Muriel was, but somehow Erin didn't like to.

"Where were your parents married? It wasn't St Marks was it?" Jude asked as though reading her thoughts.

"No it wasn't and I know Mum didn't see Muriel the other day, but that's just because she'd left, not because she's a ghost."

"Of course. It's perfectly understandable that she'd leave… odd though she didn't walk down the path past us. She must have gone the other way, into the old part of the graveyard. I expect there's a footpath or something to get out that way."

"No, actually there isn't…"

Jude grinned. He was teasing her, wasn't he?

"So, we invite her? Instead of standing at the back she can have a seat in the congregation and instead of standing aside when pictures are taken she can be in one and we'll give her a copy to keep and instead of waving everyone away she can come to the reception too."

"OK," Jude said.

"Really?"

"Yes, really. Either you're right and she's a normal old

lady who likes watching weddings and will enjoy ours, or she actually is a ghost. In that case she's a ghost who likes weddings and will enjoy ours. Hey, maybe it will put her soul to rest?"

Erin wrote out the card and took it with her to church the next time she visited her parents. After the service she gave it to Muriel. "I do hope you'll come and of course you can bring a friend or someone if you like."

"Oh, that's so kind of you. Thank you so much. Yes, we'd both love to come."

Erin grinned at the old lady's delight. She was so glad she'd thought of asking her. The idea of Muriel standing at the back watching would have unnerved her, but her coming as a guest seemed different.

"What happened?" Jude asked.

"Sorry to disappoint you, but her hand didn't go through the invitation. She took hold of it and said she'll be coming and bringing a friend. I think that proves she's real."

"Or a poltergeist. They can touch things, can't they? I wonder if her friend will be very young, but wearing a very old uniform."

"Even if he is and you're proved right, which I doubt, I'm still not saying obey in the wedding vows."

He gave a mock sigh. "All right, but every year on our anniversary you'll have to admit I was right and you were wrong."

"OK, but only on that one point."

They kissed to seal the bargain.

As Erin walked down the aisle on her father's arm, she looked at all the people who'd assembled to share their special day. Her and Jude's families were all there and many of their friends, new and old. Muriel sat halfway down, wearing a fabulous multicoloured dress and hat. She looked very real, sitting there next to a friend of Mum's.

The service went perfectly. Even better than Erin had imagined. Neither she nor Jude stumbled over their vows, the rings slid easily onto their fingers. Her brother gave the reading in a clear voice. The flower girls behaved perfectly. The guests looked wonderful and sang the hymns loudly. As Jude lifted her veil and kissed her, Erin felt surrounded in love and good wishes. When the church bells rang out joyfully to announce their marriage, Erin cried tears of happiness. She wasn't the only one.

"I love you, Mrs Anderson," Jude whispered in her ear.

"I love you too and I'm so happy to be your wife."

They posed for photos and got showered with confetti. Jude reminded her they planned to have one taken with Old Muriel. "Be interesting to see how that comes out."

The bride and groom climbed into the white-ribboned car for the short drive to the reception. They looked into the hall and said how lovely it looked, decorated with flowers and ribbons to match the bridesmaids' dresses and Erin's bouquet. She nearly cried again when she saw her gorgeous cake and the name tags at her and Jude's places.

"Come on then, wife. We'd better get ready to receive our guests."

Muriel was right at the end of the receiving line. Erin spotted her as she greeted Jude's work colleagues. She welcomed and kissed them almost automatically as she wondered about Muriel and the man with her. He looked about Muriel's age. A brother? A friend who'd never been more because her heart still belonged to her dead fiancé?

Muriel kissed Erin then Jude. Her companion shook their hands.

"Thank you so much for inviting my husband and I," Muriel said. "We were so pleased to come. We attend a lot of weddings of course, but not often as guests. This has been such a nice change."

Erin didn't dare look at Jude, but she guessed he'd look as confused as she felt.

"Wonderful," Muriel's husband said. "You know, Muriel love, I was thinking we could get our wedding blessed and have a proper reception and service. Would you like that?"

Muriel's face showed she would. Erin doubted she'd looked any happier when Jude had proposed and she'd been ecstatic then.

"So you were married, just not in church?" Erin asked.

"That's right, dear. Harold was called up before we could have the wedding we planned, so we had a quick registry office affair."

"I see, and you watch other weddings because you missed out?"

"And because I like to walk down with Harold too."

"Sorry we were a bit late getting here," Harold said. "I had to change first. This suit's just a bit too tight for bell ringing in and I wanted to be sure I did a good job for you both."

As they took their places at the head table Erin asked her new husband, "What will you tell me every year on our anniversary?"

"That I love you."

"And, I was right and you were wrong?"

"Yes, but only on this one point."

23. Working With Mr Heath

It was no good, Janie thought as she followed her boss into work at Horror Effects Incorporated, Mr Heath would have to die. He'd annoyed her just once too often.

She'd overlooked the way he always 'accidentally', let the door go in her face whenever she followed him anywhere, telling herself that perhaps he really hadn't seen her behind him. This time he couldn't get away with that as he'd just spoken to her, so he stood aside to let her through before him.

"Thanks," she muttered through gritted teeth. Maybe she'd let him have a quick death, but he still had to die.

"I am sorry, Janie. The mistake is entirely mine," he finally admitted in the lift.

That much was obvious, so saying so wasn't particularly gracious of him, especially as she was the only one to hear his apology. She seethed as she remembered how, when one of the men made a small mistake, Mr Heath tactfully returned their work for correction. If the error were Janie's he'd let everyone know so they could learn from it. Until now, she'd thought maybe it was intended as a compliment. Perhaps his intention was to show that attention to detail was vital when even someone as thorough and competent as Janie could occasionally get something wrong.

As they stepped out of the lift, Mr Heath said, "Sit yourself down and get warm." He moved the heap of dirty rags off a chair, then dragged a heater across the room and turned it on full. "I'll put the kettle on."

OK, maybe death was a bit harsh. Perhaps just a severe maiming would be enough to punish him? By the time he'd brought her a mug of tea and a chocolate biscuit, she was thinking more in terms of a painful illness.

He never usually offered any help when she had to move anything heavy and often gave her the dirtiest jobs, but that could have been his way of showing he valued her just the same as the men.

Mr Heath stood close behind her as she sipped her drink. He often stood looming over her shoulder while she concentrated on a complicated task. Perhaps he supposed he was offering moral support rather than being intimidating.

Janie was still having trouble seeing any positive side to his latest action though. She'd been a little wary when he first suggested she might like to act as host for a visitor they were expecting to tour the company's premises. Then Mr Heath had told her the visitor's name.

"Oh yes! Yes, I'd love to. I'm a huge fan, I've seen every one of his films. He really is a talented actor."

"Quite." Something in his expression told her Mr Heath didn't want to hear every detail of her crush.

"It is the famous actor who's coming and not someone else called Angus Beaumont?" she asked.

"It's the actor. He thinks coming here will help him prepare for his next role, apparently. You would have to come in early, show him round and explain everything we do here."

"No problem."

"Then in the evening, I plan to take him out for a meal. Perhaps, er, you'd care to join us? I, er, I'm sorry if this sounds sexist, but I thought having a woman join us might lighten the mood a little. I hope to entertain him as well as talk business."

"That's all right, Mr Heath. I understand."

To be fair, despite being extremely annoying in almost every other way, he wasn't sexist in his treatment of her. He never called her 'darling' as some of her colleagues did and he never expected her to make tea more often than the men did.

In fact, he was very understanding about 'girlie stuff'. Once she'd been suffering menstrual cramps he hadn't dismissed her discomfort, instead he sent her home to rest, advised she try a hot water bottle and suggested she see her doctor if she regularly suffered a lot of pain.

She'd guessed his wife must appreciate such compassion.

"I'm not married," he told her. "My sister used to suffer. Besides, if you're not feeling well, you can't work properly."

When she returned to work, she discovered he'd allowed the other men to think she'd had a stomach bug and Mr Heath assured her that if Janie needed time off work for any kind of treatment, that wouldn't be a problem.

So, she'd actually believed him when he said she could spend the day with her hero and would be treated to dinner in a fancy restaurant at Mr Heath's expense. The afternoon before she'd been so excited, she could hardly concentrate on her work. She switched her computer off just after four thirty and was out the door dead on five.

Janie got up really, really early. She had to be at work an hour earlier than usual and wanted extra time to spend on her hair and make-up, but even so, she was awake long before her alarm rang. She had plenty of time to fret about the bags under her eyes as she waited outside work. She also had plenty of time to fully experience the biting wind and stinging rain.

After an hour, a large car pulled up beside her. The electric window glided down, wafting warm air into Janie's eager face.

"What are you doing here so early?" Mr Heath asked.

Janie couldn't narrow her eyes much more as she was already squinting against the cold, but she tried.

"Oh no! You didn't know. The visit has had to be delayed until next week, something to do with a film shoot over-running."

So Janie had followed him into the building, plotting his death. By the time she'd drunk the tea he made her, a painful, lingering death seemed a bit harsh. He did still deserve to be punished though. She was still trying to think of something suitable, when one of her colleagues mentioned voodoo dolls. That sounded perfect. As soon as she could, Janie acquired red wax and formed it into a small model of her boss's head. Sticking pins in it was traditionally the next step, she knew but she couldn't quite bring herself to do that. Instead, she made a few light scratches.

At work the next day, Mr Heath's face did seem slightly red and, on a couple of occasions, Janie noticed him scratching his cheeks. She couldn't be sure that any change wasn't all in her imagination though.

She might have left things there, but later in the day he stood looming over her again. After he moved away, she noticed one of his hairs had fallen onto her desk. Later, she wrapped it tightly around the top of the model head she'd made.

The next day, Mr Heath's face was much redder and he constantly scratched as his face and scalp.

"Are you OK, Mr Heath? You look a bit red," she said.

"My skin is itchy. I think I might be reacting to my aftershave."

"Could be." Janie had noticed he'd started using it recently and that explanation seemed more likely than Janie having developed magical powers.

Throughout the day, Mr Heath became increasingly uncomfortable. His skin was almost the exact shade as the wax Janie had used on her model and where he'd been scratching, he had marks on his face corresponding with the scratches she'd made.

It wasn't just Mr Heath who was feeling uncomfortable. Janie needed to prove to herself she wasn't responsible. When he was away from his desk, she grabbed her opportunity. His sweater was draped over his chair, with a tempting loose thread. Janie snipped it off. She used more wax to give her model a body, which she then tied with the thread.

The following day, Mr Heath's whole body itched and the scratches on his face had become angry red welts. Remembering his compassion when she'd felt unwell, Janie went to speak to him.

"I think you should visit your doctor as soon as possible. If you go now you might get an emergency appointment."

"But I have so much to do," he gestured to his desk.

"I'll take care of it."

"Thank you, Janie. I really appreciate your kindness."

She did complete his work as she'd promised, but not until she'd got hold of more wax, in a cream colour this time, and made another model of Mr Heath. She worked it very gently and kept it with her. During the next two days, she regularly stroked the face with what she hoped were soothing gestures. Strangely, as she did so she began to feel affection for it and to think of her boss with fondness.

He rang into work and asked if she'd received his email. She hadn't. Janie hated the way her boss and colleagues communicated electronically rather than walking across the office, so she rarely bothered to check the internal system. She logged in and discovered two unread messages. One was from last week to tell her the actor's visit had been delayed. Oh! Good thing she hadn't killed Mr Heath then; she'd have felt really guilty when she realised he had tried to let her know the change of plan.

The second email was to tell her the visit was on again for the following day.

'He's short of time, so no need to come in early. Actually, ten will be fine.'

She still wasn't sure she trusted him, so came in at her usual time. Mr Heath was back at work and his face was back to its normal healthy colour.

"I'm allergic to strawberries," he told her when she asked. "As long as I avoid those, I don't think I'll have any more trouble."

"I'm sure you're right." She gently caressed the second model which lay snug in her jacket pocket.

Angus Beaumont arrived just after ten. He was perfectly charming to Janie, even if he did look at her bust more than her face. Up close he wasn't as handsome as on the television and his teeth were an unpleasant colour. Surely he could afford to have them fixed?

As Janie showed him around the premises, he appeared very interested, that is he did when he wasn't on the phone. He made and received calls almost constantly. In one he was clearly arranging to meet 'Chantelle darling' later that evening. Oh well, she hadn't really expected him to fall for her.

In another call, he thanked 'Becky sweetheart' for a wonderful night, then rang 'Fran my love' to make plans for the weekend. He disappeared for two hours at lunchtime, then returned without a word of apology or explanation.

The tour completed, Janie took their guest back to Mr Heath.

"I can't stay to dinner, so sorry," the actor informed him.

"We understand," Mr Heath said. "Mr Beaumont, before you go, we'd like to give you a memento of your visit to Horror Effects Incorporated."

"Oh, but that's wonderful," he said as he accepted the small box and removed a tiny red wax figure.

"Janie made it; she's our most talented prop designer," Mr Heath said.

"Oh, what a clever little thing you are, my dear. I hadn't realised you were one of the artists. You're so pretty, I thought you must be PR or something."

Unreliable, unfaithful and sexist! What had she ever seen in him?

"This is brilliant work," the actor continued. "I don't think anyone has ever made a wax effigy of me before."

Of him? Conceited pig. Although now she looked at him without the make-up and soft focus lens, he did look quite a lot like Mr Heath. They both had the same silky brown hair and broad shoulders.

Angus said his goodbyes and left them a signed photos of himself.

"You did very well today, Janie. Thank you." Mr Heath

smiled, showing his lovely white teeth.

"Thank you, Mr Heath."

"Call me Tim, please."

"OK, Tim. Well, I'll be off home then, unless there's anything else you want me to do?"

"No, no work, but the restaurant is already booked and I'll have to pay for the meal. Perhaps you'd like to ring your boyfriend and see if he would like to join you there?"

"I don't have a boyfriend, Tim. Why don't you take your girlfriend out?"

"I don't have one."

They stood looking at each other. Janie's hand was in her jacket pocket. She could feel the wax of the second model becoming soft in her hand.

"Janie, I don't suppose, that is, would you care to come out to dinner with me this evening?"

"Yes, I'd like that, thank you. Can you hold on a minute though? There's something I need to do first."

She returned to her desk, opened a drawer and quickly filled it with scrunched up tissues. She placed the second model of Tim gently on top. She didn't want any harm to come to it, or him.

24. Listening To Cassandra

"Will you be in for dinner, love?" Cassandra asked her son.

"Why?"

"Don't give me that look. It's an innocent enough question."

"Hmmm."

"I just want to know how much to cook."

"Sorry, Mum. I thought you'd had another of your weird dreams about me."

"I haven't! I'm making toad in the hole. That's not something you can stretch out."

"Sorry. Yes, I'll be here." He even gave her a hug before dashing off to work.

It was true, she hadn't had a dream. It was a premonition. After twenty-four years of them, she could tell the difference.

He was right about the weird part though. For once it hadn't been about him. At least, not directly.

Cassandra's first premonition came when she'd been expecting Chris. She'd known he'd be a boy almost before being positive she was pregnant.

That feeling of certainty had returned two or three times a year. Occasionally the premonitions were a comfort, such as the time Chris had a raging fever. Cassandra was distressed to see him suffering, but not nearly so worried as Martin. She knew her baby would be OK.

Often the premonitions were frustrating. What good was it to know he'd have a row with his best friend if her chat, on the way to school, about how to get along with people hadn't stopped it happening?

For Cassandra, getting along with her family included trying to keep her premonitions to herself. They didn't want to know, even when they might help.

When Chris was seven he'd had a series of nasty chest infections. Everyone listened to the doctor's prediction that keeping him warm, dry and away from people with coughs, colds and flu as much as possible would help prevent them recurring. They seemed to have cleared up by spring and Chris asked to be taken bird watching.

"Not today," Cassandra said at exactly the same time Martin said, "Great idea."

"We'll all get soaking wet," she warned.

"Is this one of your weird dreams?" Martin asked.

Ignoring that she said, "It's April. It's bound to rain soon."

"There's not a cloud in the sky," Martin pointed out.

As the others collected up their binoculars and notebooks, Cassandra made a flask of hot chocolate. She hid it in the boot of the car along with towels and warm clothes.

Throughout the, unseasonably warm, afternoon Chris and Martin teased her by pretending they could feel rain and making comments such as, "Wish I'd brought my raincoat."

They didn't laugh so much when, as the light started to fade, two idiots on motorcycles roared through puddles drenching them all in muddy water. After a miserable trudge back to the car, a hot drink and chance to dry off were very welcome.

After that, Cassandra had rarely told the others about her

premonitions, simply acting on them for the good of her son. At least she tried. One night she had a premonition he'd be hungry, so when she made up Chris's lunch box for college she added extra fruit, crisps and a bag of nuts.

He'd arrived home ravenous.

"In the park, where I normally eat my lunch, there was a homeless man. Really skinny and not much older than me. When I saw how much food I had for one meal I guessed it was probably more than he'd had all week. He looked so sad and then so surprised when I gave it to him, I'm sure it was the right thing to do."

"I expect so," Cassandra said. Being sure was a family trait, wasn't it? Fortunately she'd made an extra large batch of spaghetti bolognese, just in case her first ploy to stop her son's hunger had failed.

When she knew he'd get caught in traffic on the way to a job interview she felt she should say something. For once he listened and took a different route from the one he'd planned – and got stuck in traffic.

"You made it worse, Mum. They seemed to think it odd that I'd taken that route. I'm sure they thought I'd just heard about that hold up and used it as an excuse for being late."

"I'm sorry, love."

"Keep your weird dreams to yourself in future, will you?"

She did even when, a few months later, she saw on the news that the company concerned had closed down. If Chris had arrived on time and been accepted, he'd now be out of work and in competition with lots of others. As it was, he'd already found something else.

She kept quiet when she read the piece in the paper about the young man who'd had an alcohol problem which resulted in him becoming homeless and almost suicidal.

'At my lowest ebb a lad gave me his lunch and talked to me about his hopes for getting a qualification at college. His kindness and enthusiasm for the future helped me seek the help I needed. I'm sober now and training to be a teacher.'

As Cassandra scanned the words, she knew not only that this man would succeed, but that her grandchildren would benefit from his inspiring teaching methods. Not for a while though. Chris was still single.

Two nights ago, Cassandra had the first ever premonition which didn't directly involve Chris. She was going to lose her purse. By then she knew she couldn't stop it happening, so had removed her credit cards and everything else which would be hard to replace. She left an old receipt with her name and address inside.

Then last night she'd had another premonition. Two in a row was unusual. Even more odd, this one involved a stranger. Louise was slim, pretty, dark-haired – and walking Cassandra's grandchildren to school.

Cassandra opened the oven door to check the toad in the hole. It was almost done and big enough to feed four.

Martin said, "Smells good!"

"Thanks. Ummm let's eat at the table tonight and perhaps have a bottle of wine?"

"If you like. Shall I lay the table?"

"Please."

He didn't say anything when she handed him four sets of cutlery. He had that expression on his face which showed he was racking his brains to remember who their guest might be. Chris did much the same thing a few minutes later when Cassandra suggested he change out of his work clothes and into something nicer.

Cassandra smiled to herself. Sometimes it worked to her advantage that they didn't always listen to her. They were both busy when the doorbell rang. Cassandra opened it to see a pretty, slender dark-haired girl holding out a purse.

"I think this must be yours? There's no money or anything in it, but I found your address and had this weird feeling that I should bring it back to you."

Of course she had.

"That's very kind of you. I'd like to say thank you properly... We're just about to eat dinner. I've made rather too much toad in the hole, I don't suppose you'd like to join us?"

"Toad in the hole? I would, thank you. That's my favourite!"

Of course it was.

"Come in then and I'll introduce you to my family. I'm Cassandra by the way and you must be Louise."

"Yes. How did...?"

"I'll tell you later. There's no rush. You and I are going to have plenty of time to talk."

Cassandra knew that was true and that Louise would listen to her mother-in-law.

25. A Nice Cup Of Tea

Gladys waited for the kettle to boil and wished she were making tea for George. How many times had she boiled a kettle for him? Over sixty years ago she'd started doing it. At just seventeen, she'd been so noticeable and pretty, with long red hair, green eyes and freckles. She saw her reflection, distorted in the kettle's round metal surface, distorted too by age. Her hair was all anonymous, neat grey curls, her freckles hidden amongst the age spots and wrinkles, her once bright eyes faded and cloudy. No one noticed her now.

George had thought her beautiful at seventeen, when she'd started work at Bryce's and made him his first cup of tea all those years ago. It had been a humid, thundery kind of day. He was hot, tired, thirsty and fed up. Then Gladys had appeared offering him a drink. He'd sipped gratefully and returned her shy smile.

"You're new aren't you?" he'd asked.

"Yes, I'm on trial, I hope they'll keep me on."

"Oh they will, I'll tell them I won't drink tea made by anyone else. I'm their best bowler and the boss wants us to win the company's cricket championship this year. Don't you worry, lovey, you'll be staying."

She was indeed taken on permanently, and earned extra pay for serving tea at the cricket matches.

He'd thought her beautiful when she took him home to meet her parents and had made tea for them all. He'd still thought her beautiful when she'd made him his last ever cup. She knew because he told her.

It had been hard for Gladys those last few months. They knew the cancer he had developed at fifty could have killed him then. The treatment had saved him and they'd had many precious, fun filled years since. They had been lucky, but knew it couldn't last. That terrible disease had returned a year ago. The doctors had tried; an operation, all kinds of therapy, but this time they were defeated.

"Take me home, Gladys, please take me home."

She did. The children brought the big bed downstairs and converted the sunny dining room into a comfortable bedsit. They visited in turns, spending a few nights with their parents. They did everything, shopping, cooking, and cleaning. Everything that is except make the tea. Gladys always made his tea.

One day, just a month ago, he'd told her to send the children home.

"Let's be on our own for once."

It hurt her to look at this once strong man, now unable to stand without help. She'd held his hand and they'd talked all afternoon. She barely let go, except to boil the kettle.

"Not long now, love," he whispered.

She'd nodded, trying not to weep. "I hope the angels can make you a decent cup of tea."

"You are my angel, my beautiful angel. I'll not drink tea made by anyone else."

They didn't talk of death again. Instead, they discussed all the cups of tea they had shared. They laughed at how they'd slipped away from their own engagement party, escaped the laughing friends and sparkling wine, to enjoy a quiet cup of tea together. They remembered how after their wedding they had gone home to try out their lovely new kettle, a gift from their workmates, before setting off on honeymoon.

She remembered their third anniversary. They had gone away for a long weekend. They had seen a Romany caravan with a sign promoting a fortune teller. Gladys hadn't really wanted to go in. She'd worried she might be told their longed for children would not arrive. George had persuaded her.

"It's just a bit of fun, it doesn't mean anything."

The gypsy had looked into her crystal ball, then laughed.

"Better read the leaves for you two I think."

Gladys had been more afraid then, just for a moment. She drank the tea and felt reassured.

"Children, you want children."

"Very much," George replied as he squeezed his wife's hand. Gladys didn't dare speak.

"A girl first, beautiful as her mother, then boys, good strong boys. And tea, lots of tea. Some sadness too, but you'll drink tea together for eternity."

Well, she'd been right about the beautiful daughter, and the strong sons. Right too about the sadness. She wasn't quite right about the tea though. They didn't drink tea together now. Gladys no longer wanted it, and George was gone.

That last evening, just before they settled down for the night, George had requested another cup of tea.

"One last cup together, Gladys my angel."

They had drunk tea together, neither saying a word. When it was finished, Gladys, without even washing the cups, had climbed into bed beside her husband. They held each other tight, both comforting and being comforted. In the morning, George was gone.

The kettle boiled, recalling Gladys to the present. She wasn't sure she wanted tea, she hadn't drunk it since that last time with George, it didn't seem right. Tomorrow would have been their wedding anniversary; she hoped the hot drink would help her to sleep.

She took her cup into the downstairs room she still used as her bedroom and sat in her chair. She sipped the tea, and its warmth comforted her a little. She fell asleep where she sat.

"Gladys, Gladys my angel."

She felt someone gently shake her shoulder. She opened her eyes, George stood before her, strong and healthy. He took the cup and saucer from her hands.

"Gladys, come and make me a cup of tea. I haven't had on since the last one you made me. I told them I wouldn't drink tea made by anyone else."

She stretched out her hand to meet his. She stood up, flicked her long red hair over her shoulder, and went with her husband.

Thank you for reading this book. I hope you enjoyed it. If you did, I'd really appreciate it if you could spare the time to leave a short review on Amazon.

More by Patsy Collins

Short story collections –

Over The Garden Fence
Up The Garden Path
Through The Garden Gate

No Family Secrets
Can't Choose Your Family

All That Love Stuff

Not A Drop To Drink (Ebook only and
generally available free of charge.)

Novels –

Firestarter

Escape To The Country

A Year And A Day

Paint Me A Picture

Non-fiction –

From Story Idea To Reader
(co-written with Rosemary J. Kind)

Printed in Great Britain
by Amazon